NEXT DOOR NEIGHBORS

NEXT DOOR NEIGHBORS

By
Josephine Lawrence

Author of
THE BERRY PATCH, RAINBOW HILL
and ROSEMARY

Illustrated by
Clara Burd

NEW YORK
CUPPLES & LEON COMPANY

COPYRIGHT, 1926, BY
CUPPLES & LEON COMPANY

Next Door Neighbors

PRINTED IN THE UNITED STATES OF AMERICA

CONTENTS

CHAPTER		PAGE
I	AT SIXES AND SEVENS	1
II	THE 4.30 COMES IN	12
III	NANCY BOLTON'S DAUGHTER	23
IV	NEXT DOOR NEIGHBORS	34
V	DONALD APPROVES	44
VI	AN ACCIDENT	59
VII	THERE WAS AUNT AMELIA	70
VIII	CURLS WHILE YOU WAIT	80
IX	NOT A SUCCESSFUL EXPERIMENT	90
X	WITH NEEDLE AND THREAD	101
XI	THE DREAM HOUSE	112
XII	LELIA'S LETTER	123
XIII	ANOTHER JOB	133
XIV	THE BOROUGH COUNCIL	144
XV	THE LADY IN WHITE	155
XVI	FAIRY GARDENS	165
XVII	MARIAN MAKES A RESCUE	176
XVIII	GLORY RIVER	187

CONTENTS

CHAPTER		PAGE
XIX	Secrets	198
XX	Appointed Ambassador	208
XXI	David Tumbles	219
XXII	An Unanswered Question	230
XXIII	The Great Scheme	248
XXIV	Two Conspirators	259
XXV	In Disgrace	274
XXVI	The End of the Book	285
XXVII	Dedication Day	296

NEXT DOOR NEIGHBORS

NEXT DOOR NEIGHBORS

CHAPTER I

AT SIXES AND SEVENS

THE screen door of the Drayton kitchen, no matter how cautiously it was opened, invariably squeaked. The betraying hinge rasped now and the man at the kitchen table did not even turn his head.

"Go away," he said distinctly. "Clear out."

"Aw, Pete—" Dix Drayton's flute-like voice dripped with sorrowful appeal. "Aw, Pete, I only wanted to ask you—"

"Either come in or stay out," said the "Pete" so addressed, amending his first order. "Can't you see you're letting in flies?"

The small boy slid hastily inside. He had tousled yellow hair, and seraphic blue eyes—sea-blue eyes. He looked to be about five years old and his grin, displaying several gaps where his front teeth should have been was dental evidence that he was "going on six." His face was extremely engaging and exceedingly dirty.

"Is dinner 'most ready?" he asked, leaning against the table.

Peter Parsons surveyed his visitor grimly. He even pushed up his steel-bowed spectacles, the better to get an unobstructed view, though his acquaintance with Dix dated from the day of the lad's birth. A spare man was Peter, immaculately tidy, a little past middle-age and with a perpetual crease between his near-sighted eyes that led strangers to suspect him of crossness. This was an injustice though, to be sure, he had a sharp tongue. Peter was fond of saying that you couldn't live in a house with three harum-scarum boys and a father who never put foot outside his study, without needing your voice. Peter used his voice and used it with good effect. But he was not irritable and Dix knew he was in reality as tender-hearted as the father who could never say "no" to anything his sons might propose.

The kitchen in which Dix and Peter faced each other was whitely scrubbed as to floor and table and every utensil in sight polished till they reflected the light. Yet everything was in a curious disorder. Nothing gave the idea that it had a place of its own and the general effect was one of confusion. The casual beholder might have been at a loss to fathom the reason, but a little knowledge of the Drayton family affairs would have set him straight. This was a man's kitchen, in a man's household, and no womanly hand ever brought order out of the chaos.

"Dinner?" said Peter Parsons now. "Do you know what time it is? Half past three. Anyway, there isn't going to be any dinner," he added with the finality that Dix knew intimately.

"Aw, Pete, aren't we going to have anything to eat?" the small boy urged. "Has Dad a headache? Why aren't we going to eat?"

Peter turned to the editorial section of his newspaper and prepared to enjoy a long political discussion.

"Your father is going out to dinner—and you kids get bread and milk in the kitchen," he announced.

In his way Peter was far more an autocrat than the haughtiest cook. He knew he had the Drayton family under his thumb and while he loved them collectively and individually, he thought it for the good of at least three of them, to be kept in a more or less submissive state.

Dix had all the small boy's share of curiosity.
"Where's Dad going?" he asked eagerly.
"Next door," said Peter with brevity.
"Next door? Over to Bolton's?" babbled Dix. "Why? Is Donald invited? Can Dave and I go?"

"No one is invited but your father," Peter informed him. "Can't the Professor go out to dinner without upsetting the family? You'd better go wash your face and hands," he added without changing his tone.

This was a familiar suggestion and Dix paid little attention.

"Why is Dad going to Bolton's?" he persisted.

Peter looked exasperated, but he was secretly pleased. He had the human trait of liking to be the first to impart a piece of news.

"Mayor Bolton," he told the eager-eyed lad, "is at sixes and sevens. His nephew is coming to visit him."

Dix precipitated a perfect avalanche of questions. Why was Mayor Bolton at sixes and sevens? What was the nephew's name? How old was he? Would he live next door? Did Dad know him? How soon could the boys go over and see him?

"I don't know any more than I've just told

you," said Peter shortly. "Go wash your face and hands."

Dix started, not for the sink but for the door and there ensued the not unusual struggle in which Peter pursued and captured him and dragged him, protesting at every step, to the faucets, where he scrubbed and polished him. When Peter was on his feet it was noticeable that he walked with a pronounced limp, but this did not interfere with his agility. Dix fought viciously and tearfully until he was deposited, damp and clean if crimson and inarticulate with rage, on the back doorstep.

Then he suddenly simmered down and went around to sit on the front steps and meditate.

Perhaps the peacefulness of the scene on which his sea-blue eyes rested had something to do with his calmer demeanor. Euclid Avenue was Stillwell's finest old street and the four or five blocks comprising it, the heart of the residential section. The curbs were lined with elms that met in an arch across the road and another row of trees bounded the unbroken line of fenceless lawns, giving one long vista of magnificent old gardens. The houses were all large and old-fashioned in architecture and many of them so densely set about with shrubbery and trees as to seem almost gloomy. Some, as in the case of Professor Drayton's property, were sadly in need of paint and repairs, but this was more apparent in winter than in summer, when the vines and foliage and wealth of flowers more than made up for any defects. The Drayton grounds had too much shrubbery and the tall pine trees might have been thinned out with benefit to the lawn, but in spite of traces of neglect it was dignified and stately and the small boy on the sagging steps seemed to sense something of its still peacefulness.

In contrast to the rather somber house and grounds, the place next door—divided from the Drayton premises by a thick hedge—was in perfect order. The house was shingled, boasting large screened porches and a sweeping drive that cut a half circle in a brilliant lawn blazing at discreet intervals with many well-kept flowerbeds. There was a glimpse of a garage at the rear—the "back yard" of the Drayton's boasted only a tumble-down barn—and prosperity and efficient neatness shone from every corner and angle. This was the residence of Mayor Cornelius Bolton, whose daily life was as well-ordered and punctiliously scheduled as his outward estate. In passing it may be remarked that the life of his scholarly friend and neighbor, Professor Frederick Drayton, was as great a contrast as that offered by the two houses.

"Got anything to eat?"—a boy about fourteen came across the grass, dragging a bat after him. He asked the question more as a greeting than for information, evidently, for he did not wait for a reply.

"I know something you don't, Don," said Dix importantly.

"Bet you don't."

"Bet I do."

Donald Drayton dropped down beside a syringa bush and composed himself in an attitude of rest. Dix, he knew, was incapable of keeping a secret long.

"Mayor Bolton," announced the younger boy, "is at sixes and sevens."

"Old stuff," Donald murmured. "I knew that."

"Do you know his nephew is coming?" asked Dix hopefully.

"Nephew nothing," was the inelegant reply to this. "She's a girl. Her name is Marian."

"Pete said she was his nephew," insisted Dix, heedless of his pronouns.

"Pete doesn't know everything," Donald returned.

"No more do you," said someone sulkily.

The owner of the voice vaulted lightly over the hedge and rolled on the grass near Donald. He was a boy, three or four years younger, a lad with the "Drayton nose and chin," features by which the Stillwell citizens liked to claim they could identify any member of that family.

"Dave, did you know Mayor Bolton's nephew is coming and he is at sixes and sevens?" asked Dix with a rush.

"It's his niece," Donald explained. "Dad's going over there to dinner."

"Why?" said David curtly.

"Oh, the mayor's all steamed up," Donald asserted carelessly. "He likes to talk things over with Dad, I guess."

"Well, I don't care if an orphan asylum's on the way," said David in his sulky voice. "Let's go out to the barn and see if we can patch the flying rings."

The nephew-niece controversy was dropped by general consent and they tore off to the dilapidated barn which was gymnasium, play-room and machine shop by turn.

"If you ask me," observed Mrs. Annabel

Carey, who was rocking comfortably on the screened porch that opened to Mayor Bolton's dining room, "I'd say that it's a living disgrace the way those boys are allowed to bring themselves up."

Miss Hope Palmer, who was calling on Mrs. Carey, the Mayor's housekeeper, had not asked, but she knew the duties of a visitor.

"It's awful, isn't it?" she murmured. "And their mother was such a lovely, quiet woman. Perhaps a little girl will have a good effect on them."

Mrs. Carey shook her head darkly. It was plain to be seen that the future, as she saw it, was not brightened by the suggestion.

"I don't blame Mayor Bolton, not a mite," she said, rocking vigorously and apparently resuming the thread of a previous conversation. "The poor man is as near distracted as I've ever seen him. Nothing to go by, Miss Palmer, but this telegram saying, 'Marian Blessing arrives 4.30 train from Villyea, Wednesday. Please meet her.' And the Mayor not hardly knowing he had a niece by that name. I don't believe he's heard twice from his sister since her marriage."

"Well, it might be worse," declared Miss Palmer who was an optimist by nature. "This

Marian might have been a boy and then he would have had his hands full. Imagine another boy turned loose in this neighborhood with those young Indians next door."

Mrs. Carey sighed. It was very hard to make her friend understand."

"I guess you don't remember Nancy Bolton, do you?" she said. "This Marian Blessing's mother. Well I do and there are plenty in Stillwell who will never forget her. She was a madcap all through school—there wasn't a trick played, that she wasn't at the bottom of it; there was no holding her—the Mayor's her half brother, you know, and he was twenty years older. He tried to keep her in order, but she would laugh in his face and the minute his back was turned, she'd be off. She never did anything to be ashamed of, but she was within an ace of being expelled from school every year she attended. But she had a way with her, and for all her hot temper and willful ways, you couldn't hold out against her."

"She was pretty, wasn't she?" asked Miss Palmer wistfully. "I've always heard she was pretty—brunette, I believe."

"Pretty!" Mrs. Carey's scorn was withering. "Nancy Bolton was the most beautiful creature you ever laid eyes on! She had eyes like black velvet pansies, and cloudy black hair that was down to her knees and made a rope around her head when she twisted it up. She had the loveliest color I ever saw in my life, and the smallest even white teeth. She was a raving, tearing beauty if there ever was one—no wonder she turned the heads of every boy in town. But she ran away with John Blessing and she never came back to Stillwell, not once after that."

"Was he handsome—the man she married?" asked Miss Palmer with respectful curiosity.

"How do I know? No one in this town ever saw him, that I ever heard tell of," Mrs. Carey rasped. "She met him at some of the University teas."

"Does Marian take after her mother?" Miss Palmer ventured presently.

"I'm not saying, for I don't know," answered the truthful Mrs. Carey. "But take my word for it, that is what is worrying the Mayor; a girl like Nancy Bolton can't help upsetting a quiet house like this."

CHAPTER II

THE 4.30 COMES IN

THE light from the full May moon flooded the shabby porch and drenched the three little figures sitting in huddled attitudes, on the top step. Professor Drayton, coming up the grass-grown path—he always followed a path if there was one, and never walked across a lawn, even his own—did not see them until he was almost upon them.

"My dear children!" he said in evident surprise.

"Dix wouldn't go to bed," Donald explained, "and we're keeping him company."

"Where's Peter?" asked the Professor, some hazy notion of discipline suggesting an appeal to authority.

"Lodge night," the laconic David put in.

"So it is—" the Professor mounted the steps and sat down in one of the paintless old rockers.

Dix scrambled into his lap and the two other boys shifted their positions until they were close to his feet. The Professor's face was very white in the moonlight and there were lines in it that, taken with his white hair, would lead a stranger to characterize him as "old." His eyes were sad, but his mouth was humorous and his tall, thin figure was, as Mrs. Carey liked to observe, "as straight as an arrow." His sons were proud of their aristocratic-looking father, though they did wish he would dress more as Mayor Bolton did.

"Was the Mayor at sixes and sevens?" demanded Dix, settling himself comfortably, with much burrowing and an utter disregard of his father's best trousers.

Professor Drayton considered. His years in the classroom made him disinclined to answer the slightest question hurriedly.

"I think he was a little perturbed," he admitted.

"Is his niece coming?"—now it was Donald's turn.

"Nephew!" cried Dix stormily.

"Cornelius expects his niece, little Marian Blessing to-morrow, I believe," the Professor stated mildly. "It has been years since I have seen her."

Even David sat up at this and Donald stared.

"Why, Dad, do you know her?" he asked in

astonishment. "I thought she was new to Stillwell."

"I'm afraid I am thinking of her mother," apologized his father. "Nancy Bolton was in my classes—a beautiful girl. Not," he added regretfully, "an exceptional student, but very lovely in every way."

"Why is the Mayor at sixes and sevens?" Dix persisted.

When Dix got hold of an idea there was no living with him, his brothers said, until he had turned it inside out and back again.

"I didn't know he was," said the Professor calmly. "If he is a trifle excited or worried, that is easily understood; he has never seen his sister's little girl and he wasn't prepared for her coming. I understand that he has not seen his sister since her marriage, some fifteen years ago— Nancy Bolton dropped all her old friends from the moment she left Stillwell."

"I guess the Mayor isn't crazy about having to bring up a girl," Donald surmised shrewdly. "I don't blame him, either—you can't do a thing with a girl. They always get what they want by crying for it and they want to play your way and then yell murder if they see a snake or a hop toad and want to go home. If a fellow was coming next door, we could bank on some fun this summer—but a girl will spoil everything."

"Maybe she'll be nice," said Dix, who, as the youngest, still had faith in each new possibility.

"She'll dote on your curly hair," David informed him ironically. "Perhaps she will comb it for you, Dix."

Dix bellowed with rage and his father, still holding him in his arms, stood up.

"Worse things could happen to you young cynics, than a charming feminine neighbor to polish off the rough edges," he told his sons. "Yet if Marian Blessing is anything like her mother, you'll need all your wits to keep ahead of her; Nancy, as I recall her, could do anything a boy could do and many things better. She was a tomboy in her teens and a beauty and a belle as she grew older. Perhaps her daughter will surprise you."

Professor Drayton was often to remember that sentence of his. He never referred to it and the boys forgot it as soon as spoken, but the Professor's sense of humor jogged his memory at inconvenient intervals. To do him justice, he was not the only one in Stillwell who had said similar things or whose thoughts had run in like channels. Nancy Bolton—lovely and young and vivacious—had left traditions behind her when she ran away to marry her youthful illustrator. Fifteen years is not long in a small town and there were dozens of folk who remembered the Mayor's beautiful half sister. The news that her daughter was coming to Stillwell to live soon spread. Miss Hope Palmer may have had something to do with its dissemination—and it happened that a larger crowd of townsfolk than usual assembled the next afternoon to see the 4.30 train come in.

Mayor Cornelius Bolton was there—looking well-groomed and indifferent to the curious eyes that watched him speculatively. Stillwell citizens wondered "how the Mayor was taking it." He was popularly supposed to resent anything that threatened to interfere with his carefully ordered existence. His fellow townsmen were proud of him, but they respected his reticence and he spent more hours over his famous collection of coins and in his fine library, than among his friends and acquaintances. His political knowledge was extensive, he was head of his firm in the city and he was unquestionably Stillwell's leading and most distinguished citizen. But there were not lacking those who said that this handsome, soldierly-looking gentleman was lonely in his comfortable home. A little niece would brighten his life and give him happier things to think of than the financial and political problems he was usually called upon to settle.

Professor Frederick Drayton was not among those present—he had long ago forgotten that Miss Marian Blessing was due on this train, or in fact that the Mayor had a niece or that she was coming to make her home with him. The Professor was writing a book that dealt with the dead languages and all his spare time—which since his retirement from active teaching was all day and often till midnight—was spent on this labor of love.

However, the Drayton house was not unrepresented. It "just happened," as Donald explained to a wondering crony, that the three boys had come down to the station. Each had an errand in that neighborhood, it developed, and once there it seemed only reasonable to stay until the train pulled in. The baggage master had three times jerked back Dix, whose purpose it was to put pins on the track and make "swords," some older lad having told him that two pins properly crossed would fuse into a little silver sword once the heavy wheels had passed over them.

"If I catch you fooling around here once more

with pins, I'll lock you in the baggage room," thundered Bill Hawker, steeling his heart against the angelic smile of Dix.

"Aw, Bill," came the familiar treble, "aw, Bill, I just want to make a sword. You cross two pins, Bill—"

The baggage master's manner changed suddenly. He thrust Dix behind him with a determined movement and motioned the stragglers on the edge of the platform to move in.

"Here she comes," said Bill Hawker competently, picking up the tongue of his truck.

Stillwell had a small station and most of the trains which stopped there were locals. But the 4.30 was the prize train, handsome, magnificent, mysterious. The 4.30 thundered through towns larger than Stillwell, but day in and day out, winter and summer, this gleaming monster stopped and panted before the swinging shingle which proclaimed to a curious world that this was Stillwell. Everyone who had company coming from any distance always urged them to come on the 4.30, and when they went traveling themselves, the residents, if possible, took the 4.30 even in instances that entailed an hour's ride to the nearest junction and a long wait there for a more plebeian train. As Mrs. Carey once said you felt as though you were somebody when the conductor helped you on the 4.30.

The long train thundered down the track now, the brakes screeched, the speed slackening. Quivering, shaking lightly, the line of cars came to a stop and a cloud of white steam flared from the engine. A trunk was lightly tossed to Bill Hawker's truck, a few boxes followed and the mail bags.

Down the steps came the disembarking passengers—a few shoppers who had spent an exciting day in the city hunting bargains; students who were commuters to the University; a few summer boarders who liked to be established before the warm weather preceded them.

"Guess she didn't come," muttered Donald to David, utterly unaware that he had revealed his motive for coming down to the station.

David grunted.

"Who's that?" he suggested, jerking his head toward a girl who was rather timidly descending the steps of the last car.

The conductor and brakesmen were well forward and the little figure had to take the long jump from the last step to the platform unassisted. She carried a suitcase that pulled her down on one side and bumped against her legs at every step she took. She looked around uncertainly as she walked, but she kept moving and presently Mayor Bolton, who had been staring at her, went to meet her.

"Are—are you Marian Blessing?" he asked her with a formal politeness that was scarcely warm enough to be welcoming.

"Yes, please," said the little girl.

The townsfolk had a chance to observe her as she stood waiting on the side platform while her uncle stowed the heavy suitcase in his car and spoke to Bill Hawker about the trunk check. They saw a slim little creature who looked to be about eleven, though subsequent information set her age as nearer fourteen, most unbecomingly dressed in a dark brown frock with a wide girdle of some black stuff that cut the small wearer in unequal halves. She had a little peaked face, shy, frightened-looking blue eyes and a thick braid of fair hair which was tied with a black satin bow. The girls in Stillwell had forgotten what hair-ribbons looked like and they stared at the fair braid, so different from their modish "bobs" with ill concealed curiosity.

Mayor Drayton, coming back from his conference with the baggage master, almost groaned as he looked at his niece. Until that moment he had not realized that for fifteen years he had carried a picture of his beautiful sister in his mind. He would have declared that he had not wasted a moment in speculating on the possible appearance of Nancy's daughter and now he found that ever since the receipt of the telegram he had been painting a portrait of a lovely young girl with magnificent dark eyes, cloudy black hair and a scarlet mouth below the pansy eyes. It did not seem possible that this colorless, even listless, child could be the daughter of such a mother.

As he turned the car down the street that led from the station, he found himself remembering Nancy as he had last seen her—all in white, with yellow roses in her hair. He had driven her to a dance at the country club—he had not had a car then—and from that dance she had run away to marry her illustrator.

"I'm sorry we didn't have a longer notice," he said aloud. "The telegram didn't give Mrs. Carey—my housekeeper—much time to prepare for you."

The blue eyes glanced at him swiftly, then away again.

"Aunt Edith was afraid you wouldn't take me if she sent it ahead," Marian explained. "She waited till she put me on the train. She has five children of her own and another was a little too much."

Her voice was clear and pleasant and her hands lay tranquilly in her lap. The Mayor was glad she didn't giggle—giggles made him nervous.

"I hope you will like it in Stillwell," he told her, uncomfortably aware that his remark might with equal appropriateness be offered anyone of the dozens of delegates who yearly called on him in his official capacity.

Marian murmured something in reply.

"Your mother spent her girlhood in this town," the Mayor went on. "I think she was very happy—I like to think she was a happy creature. When the telegram came, to say you were coming—" he broke off abruptly as they turned down a wide street.

"Here we are," he said, stopping before his spacious lawn and abandoning the discussion of the telegram for the time being. "This is your new home, my—my dear, and that is Mrs. Carey on the porch."

CHAPTER III

NANCY BOLTON'S DAUGHTER

"NO pep," said Donald, reaching under David's elbow for the rolls and narrowly missing Dix's glass of milk.

"Is there something you want, Donald?" his father asked vaguely. "What were you saying?"

"Marian Blessing, you know," mumbled Donald, whose manners certainly waited on his appetite. "We saw her—"

"The kind that screams if she sees a spider," David contributed, gloomily watching Dix, who seemed determined to transfer a certain bit of jelly from his butter plate to his bread and who, in the proceeding, had already dropped it twice on the tablecloth.

"Clean to-night, too," said Donald, referring to the cloth. "Wait till Pete sees that mess—Dad, I thought you said she was going to be a pretty girl."

"Perhaps you're not a good judge," the Professor suggested mildly. "Dix, aren't you a little more careless than usual? Don't use your fork—take a knife, Son. That's better. Have you been over to call on your new neighbor, boys?"

Donald grinned at the idea of calling and David shook his head violently.

"We happened to be down to the station," he said with elaborate carelessness. "The 4.30 came in and she got off; whisy-washy, I call her."

"Now he's upset the whole tumbler," announced Donald in a resigned voice. "Honest, Dad, you ought to make him wear a bib. Pete says so. I wore a bib when I was his age."

In the handsome dining room of Mayor Bolton, a little figure in a dull brown dress and a wide black girdle, faced him at the dinner table. It was a beautifully appointed table, as different as could be from the one to which the Professor and his three lads sat down. Peter Parsons saw to it that they had clean tablecloths and napkins, but his notion of placing the table service was more original than orderly and he himself said he saw no reason for waiting on three able-bodied boys who might be supposed to look after their father's needs.

"I'm not overly fond of walking," Peter would

say, which was as near a direct reference to his physical disability as he ever came.

The most exquisitely laundered napery graced the Mayor's table and a low clump of early roses formed a center piece. Mrs. Carey had learned to arrange flowers because His Honor demanded them, but she privately thought they "messed up" a table and neatness was far dearer to her than beauty.

It was a well-cooked dinner that Mrs. Carey served and perhaps she was a trifle more attentive than usual, coming into the dining room without waiting for the signal of the buzzer under the rug at the Mayor's place. But then the youthful guest puzzled her and she was curious to see how the oddly assorted pair would adapt themselves to the situation.

Both made a conscientious effort to become acquainted, but conversation lagged from the start. There were a number of questions Mayor Bolton wished to ask his niece, but he thought the time unpropitious for a serious talk, so he confined his observations to brief queries about her journey and harmless reports of town activities.

Marian was nervous and ill at ease and found the hint of stateliness in her uncle's manner rather alarming. She could not know that his formality was his natural habit—an explanation which perhaps accounted for the fact that his one close and intimate friend was Professor Drayton. The Mayor had many acquaintances, but his list of friends did not lengthen from year to year.

The moment dinner was over, he announced that he was going to a council meeting.

"Mrs. Carey will look after you," he said hurriedly to Marian. "I hope you go to bed early—young people need plenty of sleep."

It was then seven o'clock, but Marian assured him that she always went to bed at nine o'clock. She looked rather wistfully after him as the square-shouldered figure walked briskly down the path and turned into the street.

Marian wondered if there was something she could do to help Mrs. Carey—though that efficient soul did not give the impression that she ever needed assistance. Still, there would be the dinner dishes. Marian did not know when the housekeeper ate her dinner, but surely there would be no harm in peeping into the kitchen.

"What a lovely room!" she exclaimed involuntarily.

If she had but known it, she could not have made a more tactful remark. Her kitchen was the pride of Mrs. Carey's heart. It was modern in every detail, equipped with all labor-saving devices and decorated in cream and white. There wasn't a more cheerful room in the house and when Mrs. Carey sat in the breakfast nook, where she ate her meals in solitary state from a cream-colored "Pullman" table, she felt like a queen on her throne. She said so.

"Come in, child," she said more cordially than she had spoken yet. "I'm through dinner—I always eat mine as soon as I serve the Mayor, because I think food spoils when you let it stand."

"I thought perhaps I could dry the dishes for you," suggested Marian.

"Aren't you tired from your train trip?" Mrs. Carey asked, but reaching for a snowy dish towel at the same moment.

She did dread the dinner dishes, from spring on, as she had once confided to Miss Palmer. There was something cozy about washing dishes on chilly winter nights when the snow lay on the ground and the wind howled in the chimneys; but spring and summer evenings, for some strange reason, the customary task seemed to lag.

"No, I'm not tired," said Marian in her pleasant, even voice.

She knew how to dry dishes. Mrs. Carey could

tell that from the way she handled her towel and the polish she gave the thin tumblers before she stood them neatly on the porcelain-topped table.

"I guess you've done that before," Mrs. Carey observed.

"I kept house all last year for Daddy," replied the girl, beginning on the silver. "If I could have stayed out of school I could have learned a great deal more. But Daddy wouldn't let me."

"Do—do you remember your mother?" asked Mrs. Carey.

It was a question she had longed to have answered ever since hearing that Nancy Bolton's daughter was coming to Stillwell.

"Oh, no," said Marian—her voice was extraordinarily pleasant to listen to—"no, I never saw my mother. She died the night I was born."

"Dear, dear,"—Mrs. Carey's tongue made a sympathetic clucking noise. "I never heard that. I knew your mother when she was a girl."

Then, with the fateful perversity that leads us to say the one thing we would wish to leave unsaid, Mrs. Carey stumbled on.

"You don't favor her much," she said.

"Oh, no," the pleasant little voice agreed. "My mother was a Beauty."

Her accent on the last word capitalized it.

Mrs. Carey mopped a china plate frantically. Whatever had made her say a thing like that!

"I look like my father's people," went on Marian. "But I have dozens of pictures of my mother—and Daddy did a painting of her that is coming by express. He did this, too."

She tugged at the round neck of her frock and brought into view a slender gold chain with a large flat locket attached. Touching a spring a miniature was disclosed—a girl with pansy eyes, a scarlet mouth and masses of cloudy black hair.

"My land, could he paint like that!"—Mrs. Carey's astonishment was a naïve tribute to the artist's skill. "I should think he'd be famous."

Marian gazed at the lovely face a moment, then slipped the locket back in place.

"Daddy never painted any portraits but those of Mother," she said quietly. "He tried, but he couldn't get the faces right. He was an illustrator and drew pictures for stories, you know. And when there weren't enough stories, he drew pictures for soap advertisements. I was a great help when I was a baby," she added proudly. "You have to use babies a great deal in soap advertisements."

"My land!" repeated Mrs. Carey, who was

finding it delightful to have a companion. "I never thought of it, but now I recollect most of the soap concerns do show pictures of babies."

"Well, Daddy made beautiful pictures," Marian assured her loyally. "And he took beautiful care of me and we were very happy until he was so ill. Then he couldn't draw and we had to let the girl who kept house for us go and I did the housekeeping for a year. When—he went away, Aunt Edith came to the funeral and the lawyer said there was no money left. Being sick is certainly very expensive."

Marian was finding it a relief to have someone to talk to, also. Her uncle had not invited confidences, but despite a certain stiffness in Mrs. Carey's manner, she was naturally kind-hearted and possessed an intense interest in her fellow beings and their affairs. Now as she put the dish towels into a basin of hot soapy water, she asked who "Aunt Edith" might be.

"Daddy's sister," explained Marian. "He meant for me to go and live with her, but Aunt Edith has five children of her own. She didn't tell Daddy, but she told me that one more was a little too much. So when she found a letter in a box from Uncle Cornelius to Mother, she said I must come and live with him."

"Didn't you know about your uncle?" Mrs. Carey asked curiously.

"Oh, no," said Marian. "I never heard about Mother's people. Daddy didn't mention anyone but Mother. He told me all about her, over and over. Do you think perhaps Uncle Cornelius didn't know about me?"

"Now that is something I'll never tell you," Mrs. Carey declared, wringing out her dish towels. "Mayor Bolton is dreadful close-mouthed and not one for talking of his own affairs. He may have known Nancy Bolton had a daughter and he may not. But this much is certain—you could have knocked him over with a feather when that telegram came."

"I had to come, because Aunt Edith bought my ticket," said Marian, apologetically.

"The trouble was, she didn't give him any notice," Mrs. Carey explained. "Nobody likes to be taken unaware."

"I think Aunt Edith was afraid Uncle Cornelius would make me stay with her," said Marian.

Mrs. Carey was not unduly sensitive, but it did occur to her that perhaps there had been something lacking in the welcome extended to this orphan girl. Mayor Bolton, she knew, was not one to make a stranger feel at home.

"We'll go out and sit on the side porch a bit," said the houskeeper. "It's early yet. You'll like it here when you get used to Stillwell."

They creaked companionably in the comfortable rocking chairs for a few moments in silence. Then Marian's roving eyes made out a figure on the back steps of the next house.

"Do any children live next door?" she asked eagerly.

"Three," was the significant answer. "Three of the wildest young Indians you'd ever wish to see. I've been at the Mayor for years to have a fence put up—they riot all over our place and won't even keep out of the garden."

"Aren't there any girls?" Marian inquired wistfully.

"No girls—three boys and their father who doesn't know whether they spend their days on their heads or their feet," stated Mrs. Carey. "That's Peter Parsons you see out on the back stoop now. He's probably left the dinner dishes for morning—the way that house is run is enough to make any woman wild."

"Does he do the dishes?" Marian asked, leaning forward to take a better look at this curious person.

"He does everything that is done," said Mrs. Carey resignedly. "Sometimes the Professor gets a girl, but none of them stay. They can't live in the same house with those boys and nobody blames 'em."

Marian meditated in silence for a few moments.

"Perhaps he was a sailor," she submitted, referring to the industrious Peter.

"Sailors can do everything like sweeping and cleaning and washing. They always do their own washing and they can iron and—and cook."

"Peter Parsons has lived in this town since he was born," was Mrs. Carey's calm refutation of this argument. "I don't know that he ever saw the ocean."

A door slammed and a small figure hurtled out to land on the back of the meditative Peter.

"Aw, Pete!" they heard a wheedling drawl, "why do I have to go to bed?"

CHAPTER IV

NEXT DOOR NEIGHBORS

WHEN Marian woke the next morning she had a confused impression that she was back in the old home in Villyea. She had been dreaming of the shabby little house there and her first impulse was to spring up and dress hurriedly, so that she might cook breakfast for her father.

Then she remembered. This large, sunny bedroom was not a part of the home she knew. She was in her Uncle Cornelius' house. The room Mrs. Carey had assigned to her was spacious—too large in fact, Marian thought whimsically, for one little girl. It was in beautiful speckless order, like the rest of the house, but the furniture was dark and heavy and stiffly arranged. That was the way the entire house looked, Marian reflected—as though it was not "used."

"I wonder if I ought to get up," she thought, wondering what time it was.

A crash, followed by a scream of rage, decided her. She ran to the window and peeped through the screen. A small boy was flat on his stomach on the lawn next door and a larger boy was tugging at his blouse with a vigor that threatened to rip the garment in two.

"It's mine—it's mine!" the younger lad kept screaming.

"It is not!"—the other boy gave a final heave to the unlucky blouse, lifted the owner a few inches from the ground and snatched something from under him.

The victor leaped the hedge, cut across Mayor Bolton's lawn and disappeared down the street, deserted at this hour.

"It looked like a baseball glove," said Marian to herself.

The boy left on the grass sat up and dug his fists into his eyes. Then he shook himself, rose and climbed wearily up the back steps. As he opened the screen door, someone within shouted, "Shut it—you're letting in flies!" and Marian heard the beginning of the lad's reply.

"Aw, Pete—"

Marian's trunk had been delivered the night before and stood in one corner of the room. Now she unlocked it and from the top tray—it was an old-fashioned affair that had belonged to her mother—selected a black and white gingham dress. There was a certain deft precision about her movements and she walked quietly and gracefully. She brushed and braided her abundant yellow hair, tied on the black ribbon and when she was finally ready, stepped out into the silent hall.

"Good morning," said Mrs. Carey, who stood at the head of the stairs. "I was wondering whether you were awake; your uncle has gone to the city and left word not to call you. He said you were probably tired from your journey."

Marian followed Mrs. Carey down stairs and had her excellent breakfast in lonely state in the dining room. She had been in bed when her uncle returned from the council meeting, but she had hoped to see him this morning. It almost seemed as though he were avoiding her.

In this she had hit upon a half truth. The Mayor had never been suspected of shyness, but in reality self-consciousness was at the bottom of his reluctance to make new friends. It would take time for him to become accustomed to the idea of his niece thrust into his home and guardianship. In addition, though he would not have admitted it, he had been disappointed to find that Marian did not resemble her lovely mother. Cornelius Bolton had been almost foolishly proud of his exquisite half sister and his imagination had persisted in picturing Marian a younger edition of the beautiful girl he had known and loved. This colorless little creature, badly dressed, quiet and shy, made him ill at ease. Of course she was Nancy's daughter and entitled to his care and protection. He would see that she was educated —there were plenty of good boarding schools— but in the meantime Mrs. Carey would have to look after her. He hoped the child would not upset the domestic schedule, for Mrs. Carey made him very comfortable and he knew that she would not lightly forgive any interruption of her orderly ways.

"Why don't you go out and see around a little?" suggested the housekeeper, when Marian had finished her breakfast.

There was the trunk to unpack, Marian reminded her. Mrs. Carey thought this could wait.

"You look a little peaked and I think the fresh air will do you good," she observed kindly. "School's closed—vacation started early this year, 'count of a dozen cases of measles they had over on the other side of the river. You'll find it easy to get acquainted with plenty of boys and girls."

Marian docilely went down the steps of the

side porch and crossed the lawn to the vegetable garden she saw through a low hedge. It was a flourishing garden and there was a man bending over a row of lettuce plants.

"Morning," he greeted her cheerfully. "You'll be the Mayor's niece, of course. Think you're going to like it in Stillwell?"

Marian had the feminine trick of answering one question with another.

"Did you know I was coming?" she asked.

"Sure—whole town knew it," the man assured her.

Over the wide thick hedge that marked the dividing line of the two properties, a touseled yellow head appeared.

"Hello, Mart," said Dix, with his engaging grin.

"Hello, yourself," Mart replied briefly. "Here's one of your neighbors—" he stopped and looked expectantly at Marian.

"I'm Marian Blessing," she said simply.

Stillwell was a democratic community and labor problems were reduced to a minimum inside its limits. As is the case in many of the older towns some of the "first families" had the least money, and while they very sensibly went to work, they lost nothing in social position. Mrs.

Carey traced her ancestry back to the Revolutionary heroes who had settled Stillwell and Mart Powers, who was weeding the Mayor's lettuce plants, was one of the most highly respected citizens. It never occurred to him to address Marian as "Miss."

"Well, Marian," he said genially, "this is Dix Drayton, the biggest imp of mischief you'll ever have the bad luck to know. The only two who ever come up to him, when there's mischief brewing, are his brothers—Don and Dave."

Dix beamed at this introduction as at the choicest praise and stared calmly at Marian.

"Are you going to live here?" he asked her.

"Yes," nodded the girl. "Yes, I think so. With Uncle Cornelius. You haven't any sisters, have you?"

Dix shook his head in violent negation. He conveyed the suggestion that he could manage quite happily without sisters.

"Is Mrs. Carey washing to-day?" he demanded with apparent irrelevance.

Marian was bewildered, but Mart had an intimate acquaintance with his youthful neighbor.

"She is not," he said with emphasis. "What's more, the next time Effie Needles comes to wash, she's going to lock the laundry door. And Pete says if he ever catches you anywhere near that washing machine he'll see that you get something to remember."

When Mart spoke of the washing machine, he did not refer to the capable Effie who did the laundry work for the Mayor's household. Instead he had in mind the electric washer which, reasonably enough, possessed a fatal attraction for Dix. It seemed impossible to make him understand the element of danger and he had to be forcibly restrained from poking small investigating fingers into the mysterious cogs and wheels.

Dix looked disappointed at the intelligence of an inoperative laundry and dropped down out of sight behind the hedge with no word of farewell. This, Marian was to discover, was characteristic of all the Drayton boys: they wasted few words.

"Nice kid, but he runs wild," commented Martin. "There's the garage—you haven't seen that, have you?"

Marian obediently passed on to inspect the garage. She had the curious feeling that she was in the way if she remained longer than a few minutes in one spot. Everyone had something to do, even Dix. Well, she had her trunk to unpack; she would go in as soon as she had seen the garage.

As points of interest, a garage cannot compare with a barn and Marian would have found more to see in the ramshackle structure that graced the rear of Professor Drayton's yard, than in the neat brick building which housed her uncle's two cars—a coupé and a sedan. She glanced at them dutifully, sniffed the compounded fragrance of gasolene and oil, and went back to the house.

Mrs. Carey was running the vacuum cleaner in the library and Marian found it easy to reach her own room without being seen. She was eager to see her treasures again and she made up the bed quickly, with the deft, sure motions that characterized her and then opened the trunk and lifted out the two trays.

She had few frocks and every one of them was serviceable in the extreme, drab, dark-colored stuffs that undoubtedly would "wear like iron." The middle tray held the pictures of her mother and the treasured keepsakes that Marian placed hastily in one of the drawers of the bureau, feeling that she did not want other eyes, however friendly, to appraise them and ask the inevitable questions.

The pictures—photographs, pencil sketches and one framed water color in a swinging easel frame, she arranged on the broad white shelf between the two windows. There was one photograph of her father, taken at the time of his marriage, a little thumb nail sketch of herself as a baby. The rest were all of the lovely mother and made an entrancing collection that drew the attention of anyone entering the room.

Mrs. Carey, coming in search of Marian, saw the pictures at once.

"My land, they are pretty, aren't they?" she said heartily. "I declare I can see your mother as she used to look this minute—she had a red sweater she used to wear skating. All the boys in town were crazy about her and it's no wonder. And when she went to the University it was the same thing over again—Professor Drayton could tell you that."

"The one who lives next door?" asked Marian eagerly. "Did he know my mother?"

"Of course he did—she was in his Latin class," Mrs. Carey replied. "The girl he married was your mother's best friend, too—a pretty little thing, about half his age."

"That was Dix's mother then," murmured Marian. "And she died too, Mrs. Carey?"

"She died, too," Mrs. Carey assented. "Four years ago when Dix was a year old. He gave up teaching then and began to work on his book—some say to take his mind off his sorrow. But I can't help thinking he ought to give up the book and do a little work on his sons—those boys are the talk of the neighborhood."

That afternoon, Marian was to have a practical demonstration of this statement. She had taken a book—selected at random—from the Mayor's library, and a rug out to the pear tree on the side lawn. Mrs. Carey always took a nap in the afternoon and as she made the suggestion that Marian go outdoors and read and saw how readily it was accepted, she congratulated herself that the Mayor had "inherited" a niece and not a nephew. It would have been dreadful, thought Mrs. Carey, if another boy had come to join in the performances of those Indians next door.

CHAPTER V

DONALD APPROVES

MARIAN spread out her rug in the grateful shade of the tree and opened her book. She was a sociable little creature and she would vastly have preferred a girl her own age with whom to talk. Still, a book was next best and she was prepared to be interested in her selection.

She was deep in the first chapter, when she felt something on her neck that tickled. Half-absently she put her hand—there was nothing there. In a few minutes she experienced the same sensation. This time she made a determined clutch—and sprang up with a cry of terror! In her hand was something cold and wet and slimy! With a convulsive effort she hurled the object from her—and chuckles of laughter sounded behind the hedge.

Marian ran to the green barrier and peered over. Donald and Dix Drayton were rolling on the ground in paroxysms of laughter.

"Did you throw that horrid snake on me?" she asked wrathfully.

Donald gazed at her, tears of mirth flooding his eyes.

"Snake!" he gasped. "That wasn't a snake—want to know what it was? It was a pickle!"

Well, a pickle, under the stimulation of intense excitement, might feel like a snake—Marian admitted the possibility.

"It was a mean trick," she said resentfully.

"You ought to see how funny you looked," Dix informed her. "You kept reaching and reaching—and when you grabbed the pickle, you jumped almost as high as the tree."

"It was so wet and cold," shuddered Marian.

"Huh, what would you do if you saw a real snake?" Donald said contemptuously. "I'll bet you're afraid of rice and mats, too."

Dix released his infectious giggle again.

"You said 'rice and mats,'" he snickered.

"You know I meant rats and mice," said Donald severely.

"I'm not afraid of mice and rats," Marian asserted. "I don't like them, but they don't frighten me. At least not always."

"I'll bet you're afraid," persisted Donald.

"Come on and see our barn if you're not—there are lots of rats out there."

Marian was so hungry for companionship that she seized eagerly on even such a doubtful invitation. Going to see a rat-infested barn could not be called a sign of flattering hospitality, but it was better than being left to her own devices.

"You can jump over the hedge," Dix said. "Or there's a place cut through down by the garage."

Marian chose "the place cut through," mainly because her black and white gingham hampered her. The skirt was too long. The dress had been made with the future in mind and Marian was confidently expected to grow taller before the frock wore out.

She followed the two boys to the barn which was the shabbiest, dustiest building she had ever seen. Great cobwebs were laced across the dirty windows, nailed fast even in this month of May, and more cobwebs were draped from the rafters. The main floor was evidently used as a kind of gymnasium by the boys and crude apparatus depended from the beams. An old mattress lay on the floor, presumably to break the tumbles of ambitious performers.

"We have a club house upstairs," said Donald, and led the way up a rickety ladder that threatened to collapse at every step.

The loft of the old barn had been rudely partitioned off into two rooms and there was a third and smaller one, more painstakingly constructed which had at one time served, so Donald said, as a harness room. It had one window and a tight floor, while the other two rooms retained the loose flooring of the original hay loft.

"We have meetings and things," explained Dix, suddenly awakening to the duties of a host.

"We had a barn at home," Marian told him. "And a black horse, 'Clover.' But we had to sell her a couple of years ago."

The Drayton boys, it developed, had often wished for a horse, but the barn had been "just a barn" since their earliest recollections. And Mart Powers wouldn't let them help him with the cars in the Mayor's garage—though Donald was sure that he knew everything there was to know about the interior of an automobile.

"How would you like to go up on the roof?" said Donald politely.

Marian rather thought she wouldn't care for it at all, but she was not minded to answer any plan these new friends might propose with a negative. She was too lonely to jeopardize any possible friendships.

"How do you get up there?" she countered.

"Come on—we'll show you—" the three delighted boys shouted in chorus and they sped away toward a dim corner of the loft.

There was a very small window at this end of the barn and it was open for the simple reason that not a pane of glass remained in its scarred and battered frame. Dix wriggled through the aperture and disappeared.

"There is a rope ladder hangs down the side of the roof," explained David kindly. "Of course, if you are afraid to try it—"

"No, I'm not afraid," Marian said, though there was nothing of the tomboy in her, and climbing the roofs of barns was not proving in the least attractive to her.

She managed to raise herself to a sitting position on the window sill. She looked down and saw the pear trees under which she had been reading. She looked up and there was Dix grinning at her from the ridgepole of the barn. As she glanced up he flung the rope ladder down to her and it narrowly missed flicking her in the eye. Marian began to have an intense sympathy with Peter Parsons, who lived with these boys, and with Mrs. Carey, who had to live next door to them.

"Go on—don't be all day," urged Donald's voice.

Marian reached out and began to climb the clumsy rope ladder. She expected every minute it would give way, for she was sure it was a home-made affair and she put no faith in the Drayton boys' knots.

However, the ladder held and in a few moments she found herself beside Dix. The roof of the barn sloped and after you reached the top there was nothing to do—as far as Marian could see, but to fall down the other side.

"Gee, you can climb pretty good," said Dix, being more prodigal of praise than his brothers.

David was waiting for the rope and Marian lowered it carefully to him. He joined them swiftly and after him came Donald.

"I wish Peter could see us now!" chuckled Dix, a wish that Marian could not echo.

For the first time she considered what her uncle—or Mrs. Carey—might think or say if they saw her seated on the roof of the Drayton barn with the three Drayton boys.

"Mrs. Carey would say there were four young

Indians," thought Marian, wondering if it would be etiquette to suggest that they go back.

"Donald fell off of here once and broke his arm," Dix remarked conversationally.

"Well, I was only a kid," apologized Donald.

David had been busy with something and now he glanced at Marian, his face a mixture of bravado and impudence.

"The ladder fell off!" he told her.

She did not grasp the significance of this statement, but Donald did at once. His eyes flashed angrily.

"That's a dirty trick!" he cried passionately.

"Do you mean the ladder is gone?" Marian asked a bit uncertainly.

"He untied it," declared Donald bitterly. "He thinks it would be smart to have you climb down the roof without anything to hang on to. You go down and get that ladder, Dave Drayton, or I'll make you."

"Go yourself—I won't," muttered David.

Marian had wild visions of a quarrel between the brothers and of both rolling to the ground to be mashed to a jelly.

"I can climb down—I'll be all right," she assured Donald. "If I go slowly I can't possibly slip."

"You stay where you are!" Donald barked at her. "Dave, you go get that ladder. Go before I push you off."

"Peter will come out," said Dix warningly.

"Let him!" retorted Donald. "Dave has to go get that ladder."

But Marian had no desire to be seen in such a ridiculous position. She fathomed that David would go after the ladder if his pride could be salvaged in some way.

"David, will you go get the ladder just so no one will see me up here?" she asked coaxingly.

"You know it looks silly for a girl to be on top of a barn—I feel like a Mother Goose verse," she added rather incoherently.

David's sullen face cleared a trifle.

"I'll go get it for you—so no one will see you climbing down," he said. "But Donald can't make me go."

Marian gave Donald a glance that implored him to keep quiet. David scrambled down the sloping side of the roof, dropped to the ground without breaking any of his bones and in a few minutes was back with the rope ladder.

He fastened it in place and Marian made a safe, if awkward return to the window, and through that to the loft. She noted half absently that Donald and David had dropped hostilities as quickly as they had entered upon them. Boys, Marian decided, "made up" more easily and with less formality than girls who might quarrel among themselves.

"Let's go outdoors," suggested Dix, and they turned to the ladder that led to the barn floor.

Marian had forgotten about the battalion of rats that was supposed to overrun the barn and Dix had forgotten, too. But the mischievous Donald kept his original motive in mind and he waited till Marian was at the head of the ladder and ready to go down.

"Look out—there's a rat!" he shouted, at the same moment shying an empty tin can across Marian's foot already poised to take a step.

His voice startled her and the flying can completed the shock. She tried to jump backward, slipped on the worn edge of the loft, lost her balance and to Donald's horror pitched forward and rolled down the ladder to the floor below.

"Get out of the way!" he barked at Dix, who was rushing for the ladder and, pushing his brother back, Donald scrambled down and bent anxiously over the little heap at the foot of the ladder.

"I'm all right," Marian gasped. "I'm not a bit hurt."

She sat up, to Donald's relief and though the breath was pretty well shaken out of her, it was evident that she had broken no bones. Her arms were scratched and she was later to discover bad bruises on either knee, but she was eager to demonstrate that she was uninjured.

She stood up, but put out a steadying hand for the ladder—the barn went around in unaccountable circles. She smiled wanly at the anxious-faced Donald and at Dix, who had tumbled down the ladder and now stood beside his brother.

"I'm perfectly all right," said Marian. "I just feel—a—little queer."

To Donald's relief and intense admiration, she did not cry. He knew she had had a bad fall and if ever an indulgence in tears was permissible, an occasion like this would seem to furnish a reason. But Marian just clung to the steadying ladder and tried her best to smile reassuringly.

"Say, you're all right," Donald told her awkwardly. "I didn't know you were going to fall off the loft—I was just fooling."

"I know," said Marian. "Only you frightened me when you shouted."

"Were you afraid it was a rat?" Dix asked, wondering how it must feel to fall without the mattress under one.

"Was that what he said?" returned Marian. "All I heard was, 'look out!' and I guess I leaped before I looked."

The dizziness was gone now, and when Dix suggested that they go and see if they could find any apples, she could walk almost naturally, despite the twinges in her bruised knees. Dix's experience dictated something to eat after every calamity.

"It's too early for apples," said Donald tolerantly, "but I'll tell you what—I'll dig up a radish for you from my garden."

He said this with such manifest pride that Marian sensed she was the recipient of an unusual favor, and tried to be correspondingly grateful.

Donald's garden was a small patch behind the barn and his chief crop seemed to be the radishes mentioned. He examined a number of plants before he found one he was willing to sacrifice and Dix hovered at his elbow like a youthful attendant serving in a ceremonial rite.

When Donald had selected his radish and washed it at the faucet used as a hose connection, he scraped it carefully with his broken-bladed pocket knife.

"There!" he said finally, presenting the pungent vegetable to Marian who ate it politely and tried to disguise the fact that it burned her tongue unmercifully.

As a matter of fact the radishes should have been picked and eaten several days before. But Donald guarded his garden jealously and resented any attempts at advice or interference. He distributed the fruits of his labors at rare intervals—Dix had had a radish when he lost a tooth and Professor Drayton had been presented with one for a Sunday morning breakfast: but Peter's suggestion that the radish crop be served at the family luncheon table fell on deaf ears. Had Marian only known it, Donald was bestowing upon her an unmistakable and unusual sign of his complete approval.

"She never let out a peep," he reminded David who came home later in the afternoon, wet and muddy from one of his many long prowls along the river bank—where he was periodically forbidden to go by Peter, a command supplemented at intervals by the similar edict of his father.

"I know she got a nasty knock," Donald went on, "and lots of girls would have been mad or cried all over the place. But she didn't say a thing and I don't believe she's told her uncle."

"She will," said David morosely. "Girls can't help telling everything they know."

It was David, in the days that followed, who persistently refused to accept Marian as a friendly neighbor. He said bluntly that he had no use for girls and he was not above going out of his way to avoid meeting this particular girl. David was admittedly the odd member of the Drayton family—if the Professor was excepted and he was only odd as he was absorbed in his book which had come to take the place of the dreams he had once cherished. Marian heard a great deal of the Professor and his book, in one way or another, but she had lived in Stillwell two weeks before she saw him.

"Marian," said Mrs. Carey one morning, "I wonder if you'd run up to the store and get a package of soap flakes. Effie is coming to wash to-day and she won't use any but a certain kind. I'm sure I don't know what we're coming to," added Mrs. Carey in majestic disapproval, "what with women coming to work at nine o'clock and ordering the brand of soap they'll use, but it seems to be the signs of the times."

By which you will perceive that no town is too

small or too old-fashioned to have its servant problem. Even in Stillwell, where the dignity of labor was more fairly practiced than in many places, the question of wages and the demands of the "day workers" and the more autocratic "maids" imported from the city employment agencies, furnished the ladies who called upon each other a never-ending topic for discussion.

Marian was glad to go uptown to the grocery store. She was familiar with the different streets by this time and indeed was fitting into her new life with surprisingly little trouble. True she and her Uncle Cornelius did not yet know each other with any degree of affection or intimacy, but if his niece did not draw his attention, she at least did not irritate the Mayor or interfere with his quiet, cultured plan of living. Mrs. Carey reported that Marian was a "biddable child and handy to help a body" and as long as the Mayor heard no complaints, it never entered his head to wonder what his niece did with her time. He vaguely supposed that girls sewed a good deal and read, and for the rest she would make friends with the neighboring children of her own age.

In less than half an hour Marian was back with the soap flakes. She supposed that the good-natured washerwoman had arrived by this time and would be waiting for the package in the laundry built in one end of the house cellar. She would take the flakes to Effie and save Mrs. Carey a trip. And just as she started down the cellar steps, Marian heard Dix's voice raised in a scream of blended pain and fright.

CHAPTER VI

AN ACCIDENT

THEN, to the excited girl, it seemed that Babel reigned. She distinguished Effie's contralto and the shriller notes of Mrs. Carey's tones, both crying out and begging someone to "Stop it! Stop it!"

"He'll be killed!" shrieked Effie as Marian dashed into the laundry room.

She thought it had taken her fully five minutes to get there, though in reality she had covered the few steps with incredible swiftness. The moment she saw them all, she realized what had happened.

In that one glance Marian received an impression she was never able to wholly forget. She saw Effie, a strong young colored woman tugging frantically at Dix, whose slim little forearm was caught in the wringer of the electric washing machine, while Mrs. Carey, her hands up to her eyes was moaning, "Stop it! Stop it!"

Now the electrical appliances in the house had interested Marian intensely for she had never seen so much housework accomplished with so little effort. She had listened while Mrs. Carey explained each appliance in detail and she had studied the mechanism with intelligence and enthusiasm. Without wasting her breath in a single scream, Marian ran forward and touched the button that controlled the current.

The glistening rollers stopped revolving and, at another touch, fell apart, releasing the little arm.

"Get his father—call a doctor!" cried Mrs. Carey hysterically. "His arm must be broken."

Effie sat down limply in the nearest chair.

"He'd been killed if it hadn't been for you, Miss Marian," she said, the tears running down her face.

Dix was sobbing with pain and fright and Marian put her arms about him.

"Don't cry, Dix—please don't cry," she begged him earnestly. "You're all right now. What doctor shall I call, Mrs. Carey?" she asked, turning to that efficient woman who, utterly unnerved, had for the time being lost her usual ability to control the situation.

"I can't stand it if his arm is broken," she declared. "And of course it is—"

"Hadn't I better take him down the block?"

said Marian. "There's a doctor there—I saw his sign."

"Would you?" Mrs. Carey asked, relief in her voice. "Doctor Armstrong has morning office hours and he must be in—will you go with him, Marian?"

"Of course," said Marian, wondering what made her knees slightly shaky. "Come, Dix, we'll have the doctor look at your arm—you'll need it fixed so you can play baseball, you know."

She dried his tears with her own small handkerchief and he slipped his uninjured hand in hers. Mrs. Carey and Effie watched them from the cellar doorway and one thought was uppermost in the mind of each—what would have happened if Marian, or someone with her presence of mind, had not come in and turned off the current?

Doctor Armstrong was a kindly middle-aged man, with the doctor's inexpressibly comforting matter-of-fact way of accepting accidents. He knew Dix and joked with him about his "exciting life." Then, in a few, absorbed moments, he had made his examination, heedless of the small boy's frantic protests and tears, and was ready with the verdict.

"Not broken," he announced and Marian

thought his smile absolutely beautiful. "He's a lucky kid, aren't you, Dix? You might have had a bad smash up. As it is, you'll have an arm like a feather pillow for a few days and you'll have to ask Peter or your father to keep wet cloths on it, but when the swelling goes down, you'll be as good as new."

He began to bathe the injured arm—already swelling to alarming proportions—with skillful fingers.

"Suppose you introduce me, Dix," he suggested quietly.

"Huh?" said Dix, so forlornly that both the doctor and Marian laughed.

"I'm Marian Blessing," she said quickly. "I'm staying with my uncle—next door to Dix—that's how I happened to be on hand."

"Then you're Mayor Bolton's niece—Nancy Bolton's daughter," affirmed Doctor Armstrong. "I knew your mother when she was a girl."

He glanced at her keenly and Marian flushed. She thought she knew what these people who had known her beautiful mother, were thinking when they looked at her like that.

"Was Dix doing the washing for Mrs. Carey this week?" asked the doctor, wrapping wide lengths of gauze around the arm.

Marian was curious to know how the accident had happened herself, and Dix, pressed for details, suddenly waxed communicative.

"I just put a towel in the wringer," he declared. "I didn't know it was going through so quick. I won't touch the washing machine again —honest, I won't, Doctor Armstrong."

"No, I don't believe you will," the doctor agreed, busily writing out a label.

He pasted it on a bottle and then surveyed his patient thoughtfully.

"You Drayton kids have to have your lessons pounded into you with a hammer, don't you?" he observed. "If you're going to make as hard work of learning all your life lessons as you've done in your brief five years, I'm afraid you've a hard time ahead of you, Dix."

This was over the yellow head and Dix gazed at him doubtfully.

"Let it go," said the doctor, putting an arm around him. "Now, Miss Marian, I'm afraid I'll have to make you my messenger, for Dix has a poor memory for details. Tell Peter, or the Professor—Peter would be better—to keep cloths soaked in this solution and constantly on the arm. If the pain keeps Dix awake to-night, have someone call me up; and you trot in and see me day after to-morrow, young man," he added, with a final pat on the curly hair.

It was a much more cheerful couple who went down the steps of the pleasant cream-colored house and Dix in particular was inclined to make light of his mishap. Mrs. Carey and Effie were so relieved to hear that the arm was not broken that they declared they meant to "go ahead" with the washing. In their anxiety, they had been unable to complete the task of sorting the clothes and Effie had been almost sure she would never be able to use the machine again.

"There's no one more glad than I am that baby child didn't get killed," she announced solemnly, "but I tell you this, Mis' Carey, I just can't do a thing if he hangs around this laundry; I'll be afraid to turn my back for one minute, long as he is anywhere near here."

"I'll take him home—I have to tell someone about keeping the bandages wet," said Marian hastily.

She had never been inside the Drayton house and now for the first time she realized that home-making was a woman's work. She and Dix went in the back way and her first glimpse of Peter's kitchen told her that the best will in the world couldn't make up for lack of intuition. Peter was as clean as wax, but he had no more idea of how to make a room attractive than had Dix. However, she was not there to criticize his interior decoration, but to see him.

"Where is everybody?" she asked involuntarily.

The house seemed strangely quiet. The kitchen door was open and she looked into a large hall which apparently ran the length of the house to the front door. It was dark and the rooms opening into it were dark, too.

"Don and Dave went off," said Dix, "but Peter is always in the kitchen when he isn't sweeping or making beds. Maybe he went to the city—I'll see if there's a note on the bread box."

Peter's system of communication had not failed. There *was* a note on the bread box. Dix puzzled over it a few minutes and then brought it to Marian.

"It's for Donald," he sighed. "I can't read Peter's writing."

"Bread and jelly and milk for lunch," read Marian aloud. "Be sure you shut the ice-box door. Take some in to your father. I'll be back on the 3.10."

"Pete goes to the bank for Dad," Dix explained carelessly.

"Do you suppose your father could be interrupted?" said Marian.

She thought that someone ought to be notified of the accident to Dix. The cloths were to be kept wet and she was afraid if she put the heavy bottle down in this queerly run household some of the boys might tip it over before they knew what the contents were for. Doctor Armstrong had said that Peter would be the one to tell, but he wasn't here and surely Dix's father ought to know what had happened. Besides she saw that under his tan Dix looked rather white and she thought his arm was beginning to pain him.

"Why of course," said that small boy in answer to her question. "My father doesn't mind being interrupted. He is very pleasant about being interrupted."

He spoke as though repeating something he had heard, but as he started down the hall, Marian could do no less than follow him.

Dix led her along the dim passageway, walking with the confidence of familiarity, but Marian found herself colliding with various small articles of furniture such as stools and tables. She was glad when Dix turned at the wide staircase and began to climb.

Upstairs it was lighter and while there were evidences of careless housekeeping and the bannister rail was coated with dust, it would have been expecting too much from one lame man to demand perfect order in this huge gloomy house.

"This is the study," said Dix, stopping before a closed door at the front of the second story hall and tapping gently.

"Yes? Come in," a voice called.

Dix stepped inside and Marian followed him. She saw a large, square room with four windows across one side, the shades run up to the top and a glare of sunshine streaming in on the motley collection of furniture. There were sofas and rocking chairs and more little tables and on every one of them was a pile of books. Some were large and some were tiny, all were in shabby bindings and the majority of them had little slips of paper sticking out between the pages, where the Professor had made notes for reference.

The room seemed warm and Marian noticed that only one window was up, a small one tucked away in an alcove, and the face the Professor lifted to them, above the mass of yellow papers strewn on the lumbering old desk top before which he was seated, looked heated and tired. But he smiled affectionately at his son and put down his pen.

"Well, Dix?" he said cheerfully.

"This is Marian Blessing, Dad," Dix accompanied his introduction with a jerk of the thumb on his well hand toward Marian.

"She lives next door," he pursued, "and she stopped the wringer."

Professor Drayton listened courteously, but he seemed puzzled. Then he perceived Dix's bandaged arm and the bottle in Marian's hands.

"Has something happened?" he asked hurriedly. "Are you hurt?"

"He put his arm in the wringer of the washing machine," Marian thought it time to explain. "But no bones are broken—we went to Doctor Armstrong and he says Dix will be all right in a few days. He wants the bandages kept wet with this—and if Dix doesn't sleep to-night, he says to call him."

Dix put his touseled yellow head against his father's shoulder.

"It—it hurts," he said softly and two big tears rolled down his cheeks.

AN ACCIDENT

The Professor turned and gathered him into his arms.

"There, there, lad, it won't hurt long," he promised tenderly. "We'll go down on the porch where it is cooler. Come along, Miss Marian—I used to know your mother and we should be good friends."

He had been staring at Marian, kindly enough, but still curiously. As she followed the tall figure down to the shady porch, Marian told herself she knew what he was thinking. She didn't look like her mother.

"If only I had dark eyes—or hair—so I would look the least little bit as she did," she told herself unhappily.

"I wouldn't care so much"— she stepped out on the porch—"if I only resembled her in the tiniest way."

CHAPTER VII

THERE WAS AUNT AMELIA

DIX was soon made comfortable, for Marian dipped the bandages in the cooling solution and when he was freshly "wound up," as she put it, he drowsed luxuriously in his father's arms.

"I suppose I ought to go home," thought Marian, rocking lazily in one of the shabby chairs which lacked half a dozen spindles in the back but still retained a serviceable pair of rockers.

Still, she knew that Mrs. Carey and Effie were absorbed in the washing and would be bending all their energies to recapture the hour lost by Dix's accident. She would not be missed if she did not return till lunch time.

"I wish you'd tell me about my mother," she said a little shyly.

Professor Drayton smiled at Nancy Bolton's daughter.

"She was the most beautiful creature I ever saw," he said simply. "She was all life and color. She used to remind me of a humming bird

—though she wasn't diminutive in any sense of the word. But she was so intense, so vivid and she had a way of darting from one interest to another that was fairly bird-like. When she came into a class-room, it was as though a burst of sunlight, or a sudden flare of music, cut through the dullness of the routine. A wonderful girl, with a character as lovely as her outward appearance."

He felt in his pocket for his glasses, remembered that he had left them on his desk, and sighed for his handicap.

"I'm so near-sighted, I cannot get a clear idea of how you look, even from this short distance," he apologized.

"Oh"—Marian breathed her favorite little monosyllable in a grateful accent. "You don't need your glasses, Professor Drayton. I am not one bit like my mother. Everyone says so. She was a Beauty and Mrs. Carey thinks I take after my father's people."

The Professor laughed and Dix opened an indignant eye.

"You may not be like your mother, as far as physical resemblance goes," said the Professor kindly, "but I do not doubt you are her daughter in everything more important than the mere external. My wife"—he hesitated a brief instant—"my wife used to say that Nancy Bolton's disposition was as lovely as her eyes and hair. My wife was your mother's chum in their college days," he added.

They talked a little longer in the pleasant shade of the porch and Dix dropped into a sound slumber. Marian heard more of her mother and gained new impressions of her Uncle Cornelius. It was difficult for her to imagine him as a gay, light-hearted young man who escorted his sisters to parties and who—actually—played a banjo.

"Cornelius and I were much older, of course," said the gentle Professor as Marian giggled at the picture of her staid and dignified uncle twanging a banjo, "older than the young people who gave most of the parties in Stillwell. But Cornelius was always younger than I in spirit. After—after Nancy went away, he changed and my wife died and the inevitable years did the rest. And now, perhaps, we smile as you do at the thought of those gay evenings."

When Marian saw Donald and David coming up the weedy walk, she guessed it must be near lunch time and though the Professor hospitably asked her to stay, she knew that from all points of view it was better that she did not accept.

As she went down the steps, Professor Drayton, Dix in his arms and the other two boys close beside him—Peter declared they couldn't be near their father without "getting on top of him"—said something that halted Marian in sheer astonishment.

"I think you're very like your mother," announced the Professor.

"But I'm not, of course," said Marian later that afternoon.

She was curled up in a wicker chair before the fireplace in the living room, and the portrait of her mother smiled down at her from over the mantel.

This picture was the one forwarded by express and when it had arrived and been unpacked, the Mayor had stared at it as one entranced.

"Good heavens, could your father paint like that?" he asked his niece, apparently unable to take his eyes from the vivid face that lighted the dark canvas.

And Marian had conscientiously made the explanation which she had heard her honest and painstaking father give to the dozens of friends and critics who had urged him not to waste his time at illustrating, if he could paint portraits like that.

"Daddy couldn't paint anyone but Mother," said Marian. "He tried, but they never came right. This picture was painted the first year he and Mother were married."

"It's Nancy—the living, breathing Nancy," the Mayor had declared. "I never saw anything like it. Look here, Marian, where did you think of hanging this portrait?"

Marian answered, a little timidly, that it had always hung in her father's room and she would like to keep it in hers.

"Yes, I suppose you would and certainly it is yours to do as you please with," her uncle answered. "But Marian, I'd like to have it hung downstairs. Here in the living room, say, where we could all enjoy it. I never saw a more appealing likeness—blest if I ever did," the Mayor murmured earnestly.

The portrait had been hung above the fireplace and scarcely a caller entered the room without remarking upon it. Those who had known Nancy Bolton invariably said the same thing—"a wonderful likeness." The frame was flat and dark and the background of the canvas had been painted in shadow. From this somber duskiness the dark-eyed beauty of Nancy Bolton stood out triumphantly, flamingly, compelling Her daughter felt as colorless as a meadow brook contrasted with a mountain waterfall, before that vivid joyousness.

"I'm not a bit like her," said Marian, unconsciously speaking aloud.

Mrs. Carey and her constant companion, her dust cloth, coming into the living room at that moment, the remark was not allowed to go unnoticed. Mrs. Carey took a dust cloth with her, from force of habit, perhaps, whether she essayed a tour of inspection or merely passed through the rooms of the house on a definite errand. There was never anything to dust, since she "did" the rooms systematically after a schedule of her own, but she was not to be seen without the faithful dust cloth ready for the emergency that never happened.

"Not a bit like who?" asked Mrs. Carey, whose grammatical foundation was not as secure as her domestic grounding.

"Like my mother," Marian explained.

"No-o, you certainly don't favor her," said Mrs. Carey, glancing at the portrait. "But it just came to me last night that you're almost the exact image of your Aunt Amelia. I knew there was somebody you reminded me of, but I couldn't place 'em: last night it came to me like that!"—

she snapped her fingers to illustrate the quickness of dawning light.

"Have I an Aunt Amelia?" Marian asked, wondering if she would ever reach the end of the list of relatives. There was always one more name popping up in casual conversations like this.

"Well, you haven't now," admitted Mrs. Carey, "and as Amelia Bolton died before you were born, I don't suppose, strictly speaking, she ever was your aunt. But if she had lived, she would have been your Aunt Amelia. She was the oldest of the family—your uncle's own sister."

"Oh," Marian said rather uncertainly.

"Do you know, I think I saw a picture of your Aunt Amelia only the other day," chattered the voluble Mrs. Carey. "In one of those old albums—wait a minute and I'll get it out."

There were three drawers, fitted with glass knobs, under the window seat, and the housekeeper pulled out one of these, disclosing a collection of books bound in embossed leather and plush. Marian dropped down on the rug beside her and her eyes began to shine.

"I love to look at albums!" she declared.

"Well, these ought to satisfy you," said Mrs.

Carey. "All the Boltons, on both sides of the house are tucked away in these books. In the days when folks weren't so mortal high-toned, they used to keep their albums on the table in the parlor, but now seems like they're ashamed to admit they have any ancestors. Lots of people send the albums up attic, but the Mayor didn't seem to care what I did with these as long as they were out of sight. So I keep them handy—I like to look at them myself, sometimes."

Marian turned over the pages slowly, stopping to listen to Mrs. Carey's historical comments.

Strangely wooden the figures, grotesque many of the forms of hair-dressing and utterly out of style the "best" garments of other days and generations. But the descendant of these men and women felt a proprietary interest in the quaint photographs and found the monologue of Mrs. Carey not only absorbing but illuminating.

"There it is—that's your Aunt Amelia," said the housekeeper, placing her hand down on the page to prevent a hasty turn.

Marian stared at the long, prim face, framed in two straight folds of hair that had never known a waving iron. Aunt Amelia looked even more mournful than the other relatives had looked and thirty years ago having one's picture taken was a solemn affair and not to be lightly undertaken.

"You have her forehead and her nose," declared Mrs. Carey. "I wonder I didn't see it before: she was a mortal plain woman, Amelia Bolton, and quiet as a mouse. I don't believe she was ever twenty-five miles from home in her life. She never seemed to do anything special: it was funny when she died—she had the biggest funeral ever seen in this section. People came from all creation and the flowers filled two wagons. She had the same nice ways you have—quiet-spoken and pleasant. She was always an easy woman to get along with."

Marian finished looking at the other photographs and replaced the album. She didn't want to look like Aunt Amelia, she told herself resentfully. She wanted to be pretty. Aunt Amelia might be as good as gold and easy to get along with, but she wasn't pretty—and not even the largest funeral ever seen in Stillwell would make up to her, Marian felt, if she was never to hear anyone say she was a pretty girl.

The door bell rang as she closed the drawer on the pictures and Mrs. Carey ushered in Mrs. Armstrong, the doctor's wife, and a "visiting girl," as the townsfolk like to speak of the strangers within their gates. There were "visiting girls" and "visiting boys" and the description was applied to those who were too young to be counted among the university students and their friends.

This "visiting girl" was thirteen or fourteen and the minute Marian saw her she knew she wanted to look like her. Lelia Mason was attractive, from the crown of her shining dark bobbed hair to the tips of her smart tan pumps. She was becomingly dressed in a frock of pongee silk and she looked cool and serene and yet ready for any fun that might be going on.

"If I had a dress like hers, perhaps I'd be pretty, too," thought Marian.

"Lelia is going to spend two weeks with me," Mrs. Armstrong was saying. "I hope you'll come over often and see her, Marian."

CHAPTER VIII

CURLS WHILE YOU WAIT

LELIA proved a decided addition to Stillwell's younger contingent. She was vivacious and pretty and possessed of the ability to make friends readily. She had an apparently inexhaustible supply of becoming dresses and she could play tennis, row a boat, dance and even roller skate, if she was so minded.

"She's got pep," said Donald Drayton, and Marian knew by this time that he could bestow no higher praise on an acquaintance.

Lelia thought that Marian was "dear and funny," and their friendship progressed rapidly. Marian thoroughly enjoyed having a girl of her own age to talk to and she constantly studied Lelia, her clothes and her hair and her ease of manner. Acting on Mrs. Carey's suggestion, she had invited Lelia to stay for dinner one evening and the Mayor had been favorably impressed with the young guest. He was glad his niece had found someone companionable, he said, and a girl as sensible and at the same time, pretty, as Lelia. It never entered the head of His Honor that his niece might be sensitive to her own lack of beauty and as for the fact that Lelia was merely visiting in Stillwell for a couple of weeks and was not, therefore, likely to afford Marian permanent companionship, that did not make any impression on his mind at all. He was an exceedingly busy man and often appeared to be listening courteously when in reality he was engaged in working out a separate problem in his mind.

"I wish I could look pretty," said Marian involuntarily one afternoon as she watched Lelia daintily cleaning her white shoes on a piece of newspaper carefully spread out to protect the rug.

Lelia did everything daintily. She was dressed for the afternoon now, except for her shoes. She had discovered an infinitesimal spot on the heel of one as she had been about to slip them on and now she was remedying it swiftly and neatly.

The girls were in the Armstrong guest chamber and Marian was also dressed for the summer afternoon. But her frock was a dull serviceable gingham, with no other bands of trimming save a stitched belt and four pearl buttons that fastened the side opening. Marian's fair, thick hair was brushed into its one heavy braid and she wore black stockings and neat black oxfords.

"You *could* look pretty," said Lelia, with a critical and appraising glance at her friend.

"Oh, no," Marian breathed in delight. "Could I, Lelia?"

Lelia put on her shoes and fastened the straps. "Yes," she said slowly. "Yes, I think I could make you look entirely different, Marian."

The seeker after beauty did not quarrel with the ambiguous sound of this sentence.

"Will you?" she begged eagerly. "Will you make me look different? Please, Lelia?"

Now nearly everyone cherishes the conviction that he or she has a special gift. Lelia intended to study costume and design as she grew older and she had a vague idea that she would "fix over" old houses or plan dresses for other girls to wear, or do something that called for a study of color and lines. It would be thrilling to practice on Marian and at the same time do her friend a good turn. If ever a girl needed a little advice on what to wear and how to wear it, Marian was certainly that one.

"You're sure your feelings won't be hurt?" said Lelia, hesitantly.

Marian was quite sure.

"I know I'm not one bit pretty," she announced calmly. "I'll do anything you tell me to do."

This was piling temptation on to temptation and Lelia could not resist the opportunity to try her theories. With an example before her, and so willing a one, how could she be expected to postpone or decline the attempt?

"What you really lack," she said judiciously, "is—is—well, suppose you sit there in that chair by the window and I'll study you."

Marian took the chair by the window and waited expectantly.

"What you really lack," Lelia began again after several minutes' scrutiny, "what you really lack is color."

Lelia herself was dark, with a pretty red that came and went in her smooth cheeks. She sparkled, too, though that, Marian told herself dolefully, she could not hope to achieve.

"I think you ought to wear something bright and striking," Lelia proceeded. "And merciful me, you can't do a thing with your hair while it is like that."

Marian jerked her heavy braid of hair over her shoulder.

"What should I do with it?" she asked humbly.

"Bob it," was the prompt response. "I can do it—I've had mine done so often that I could cut it in my sleep. Wait till I get an apron—say, this is heaps of fun!"

She dashed away to her closet, returning in a few minutes with a trim little over-all apron covering her pretty dress. Then she tucked large bath towels around the neck of Marian, carefully turning them in at the edge of her frock.

"Now unbraid your hair, but don't fluff it out," she directed. "Would you like it cut like mine?"

"Oh, yes," said Marian with flattering promptness. "Could I have that little curve and everything?"

Lelia's hair curved out gracefully on either cheek and it had been exquisitely trimmed to the shape of her head by one of the most expensive barbers in her home city. She assumed that it was a simple matter to cut hair—one took the scissors and slashed away till the desired effect was attained.

Marian sat perfectly still while the shearing was in progress. She had absolute faith in Lelia's ability to do anything she undertook to do and

MARIAN SAT PERFECTLY STILL WHILE THE SHEARING
WAS IN PROCESS.

Next Door Neighbors *Page 84.*

she confidently believed that her hair was going to look exactly as her friend's did.

So it was with a little shock that she gazed into the hand mirror Lelia handed to her some twenty minutes later.

"It—it doesn't look just like yours, does it?" the shorn one faltered.

As a matter of fact, it didn't. Lelia herself was a bit disappointed in the outcome. Marian from the back presented a jagged appearance and the curves that were to lie gracefully against either cheek stuck out fiercely like militant aigrettes. Neither girl saw anything funny in the result—this was a deadly serious matter.

"You'll have to train them," said Lelia, referring to the long locks. "Brush them every day the way you want them to go. And, anyway, I think you are the type that needs your hair curled: mine is naturally fluffy, but yours is so fine and straight it doesn't stand out."

Truth to tell, Marian's fine light hair, except for the unfortunate "curves," clung closely to her head and gave the appearance of a very meek little lamb.

"I'll curl it for you—Cousin Dora has an iron," said Lelia, and like a flash she was into

Mrs. Armstrong's bedroom and back with her electric curling iron.

"I never had it curled," Marian protested doubtfully.

"Well, you'll be surprised to see how nice you'll look," promised Lelia, screwing the iron into the plug.

She worked hard over her task, but it could not be said that the curls were like anything ever seen before. In the first place they each seemed to choose a different direction, some were a trifle scorched on the ends and others became discouraged before the end was reached and, starting valiantly as tight corkscrews, refused to curl at all before the tip was reached.

"It will look better when I brush it out," said Lelia hopefully.

No one could truthfully have accused Marian of having hair that did not "stand out," after the brisk application of the brush to her newly-made curls. Each separate hair stood on indignant end and no South Sea Islander ever displayed a frizzier head.

"I rather like it," Lelia declared, standing back to better survey her work.

Marian regarded herself in the mirror rather doubtfully.

"I do look different, don't I?" she said. "I wish my nose was a little fatter."

It was beyond Lelia's powers to change the shape of noses, but she tactfully proposed trying on one of her frocks.

"I have a red dotted Swiss that you'll look perfectly darling in," she told her friend. "We ought to be able to wear the same clothes—perhaps you can use my tan suede pumps."

The red dress fittted nicely—it was cut with a pretty square neck and elbow sleeves and as far as the style was concerned was in perfect taste and much more suitable than the garment Marian had just discarded. But the color drained every bit of vitality from the thin, eager little face and, worst of all, wiped all the lovely tints from her eyes. Beneath her frizzy hair, Marian's eyes showed weak and almost watery, contrasted with that blazing cerise.

"I'll lend you my red beads and the ear-rings, too," the generous Lelia offered. "They're lovely —my Aunt Emily brought them to me from Paris. Mother won't let me wear ear-rings, but I always keep them in the box with the beads."

She fastened the chain of choker beads around Marian's neck and, with some difficulty, screwed the ear-rings into the small ears.

"You need a touch like that—to make you distinctive," said Lelia.

There was a long mirror set into the door of the closet in the Armstrong guest room and Marian had an unobstructed view of herself as she stepped back.

"I never can go through the street, looking like this," she exclaimed.

"Well, for pity's sake, I thought you wanted to look different!" Lelia replied with a little touch of scorn.

"I didn't know I was going to look so much different," the object of her labors returned frankly.

"You look all right—your uncle will be tickled to pieces," Lelia assured her, patting the strange-looking hair affectionately. "You can go out the side way and no one will see you," she added with a touch of instinctive if totally unintended sympathy.

Marian felt like using any side entrance that presented itself and she "ducked" as the Drayton boys would have said, through the side door of the doctor's house and sped down the path that led to the street, where she hoped to make a quick dash across and gain the privacy of the tall hedge surrounding Mayor Bolton's side lawn.

Just as she reached the curb, a car drove up and Doctor Armstrong and his wife stepped out. Mrs. Armstrong gave a squeak—it might have been admiration, it might have been dismay—and the doctor said something that sounded like, "Good Lord!" but Marian continued her dash. She shot across the road and never stopped running until she was safely in her own room.

She spent the time before the dinner gong sounded, before her mirror, trying to make up her mind whether her uncle would like the way she looked or not. She thought he would—she hoped so, fervently. If red was what she needed she certainly had enough of it. And she could have wished for wavier hair, instead of such a frizzy mass. One thing was certain—she looked "different" and that for weeks had been her consuming ambition.

CHAPTER IX

NOT A SUCCESSFUL EXPERIMENT

THE Mayor was already seated at the table when Marian entered the dining room, though he rose as usual to pull out her chair. His formality always made it difficult for her to be wholly at her ease.

He was preoccupied, as he was apt to be, and at first did not notice anything unusual in her appearance. The discovery was simultaneous with him and Mrs. Carey who paused "in her tracks," as she dramatically recited it later to Miss Palmer, and who seemed in immediate danger of dropping the soup plate she was carrying.

"Marian Blessing!" thundered His Honor, staring across the white cloth at his niece in a mixture of astonishment and dismay that was not without a touch of humor, had there been anyone in that dining room to recognize it.

"*What* have you been doing to your hair?" the terrible voice demanded.

Marian felt cautiously of her frizzed locks.

"It's bobbed," she explained. "Don't you like it? Lelia did it for me."

"Did Lelia Mason trick you out in that red dress and those beads and ear-rings?" asked the Mayor.

"She loaned them to me," Marian replied. "She would have loaned me her suede pumps, but I couldn't wear them."

They had been too large and Lelia had said that, at any rate, Marian had one thing to be proud of—her feet.

"Don't—don't you like me this way?" asked Marian, a little piteously.

"Like you?" repeated her uncle. "That girl has made an out-and-out freak of you. Your hair is ruined and everything you have on is utterly unsuitable for a child of your age. Go upstairs immediately and put on one of your own dresses and comb your hair properly. Then come down and have your dinner."

Marian held in the tears as best she could, but by the time she reached the stairs they were falling like rain. She was bitterly disappointed and her hurt was not lessened by the conviction, which had been growing stronger every moment since she had left the encouraging Lelia, that she really looked worse than she had before submitting to her friend's ministrations.

She flung herself on her bed and buried her face in the cool pillows. She would have a good cry and then go to bed without going downstairs again. She never could face her uncle again that night, after what he had said.

Then, a few minutes later, she heard him calling her.

"Marian! Marian!—you're delaying dinner. Come down at once."

She went out to the head of the stairs, mopping frantically at her eyes and peered down.

"I don't want any dinner, please, Uncle Cornelius," she said faintly.

"Did you hear what I said?" now the Mayor's displeasure was not to be mistaken. "Change your dress and come down immediately."

Marian went back to her room and hastily took off the red dress, substituting the first thing she could put her hands on, which was the black and white print she especially detested. She didn't know what she was expected to do about her hair—not all the scolding in the world could put that long braid back where it had been that morning—but she seized a comb, held it under a faucet in the bathroom for a moment, then ran it, dripping, through the fateful frizzes. The result was a "slicked" appearance that made her red-rimmed eyes more noticeable than ever. She couldn't help that, she thought, with a despairing glance into the mirror; her uncle and Mrs. Carey must have guessed that she would cry.

"That's better," said the Mayor coldly, as she slipped into her place and silently unfolded her napkin. "The beads, please."

The ear-rings had fallen off among the pillows, but Marian had forgotten the beads. She unfastened them now with fingers that trembled and slipped them into her dress pocket. She made a pretense of eating the excellent dinner, but she could not talk—she was afraid she might cry again.

Mayor Cornelius Bolton did not mean to be actively unkind, but he felt a heavy sense of responsibility in connection with the guardianship of his young niece. He had not been prepared for it, but he would be the last man in the world to shirk it, once thrust upon him. During the years of his half sister's absence, he had come to believe that her marriage, or at least her elopement, might have been prevented, had he kept a stricter oversight of her time and plans. Nancy had always had her own way and it had been a willful, sometimes a foolish one. If she had been spoiled, reasoned the Mayor in the long, lonely evenings that followed her going away, the fault was his. And he was resolved that discipline should come before indulgent affection when he dealt with Nancy's daughter.

To be sure, Marian had, so far, given him no trouble at all. She was obedient and tractable and seemed to fit into the routine of his household almost as though she had been included in its original outline. But, he argued, she was her mother's daughter—Nancy's high temper and strong will must be part of her heritage. He was always expecting to see some evidence of high-spirited obstinacy in Marian's character and at the first evidence of mutiny he was determined to be ready and to put it down with a firm hand.

So he was convinced that the spectacle of a thin little girl in a violently cerise dress, with borrowed "jewels"—the Mayor thought all ornaments were jewels—in her ears, and a head that resembled nothing he had ever seen in all his well-ordered life, marked the beginning of an attempt to have her own way.

"In the morning, you'd better go to a barber and have him do something to your hair," said the Mayor when the salad course was reached. "There is nothing to be done, but to have it cut properly."

Marian said nothing, not daring to lift her eyes from her plate, for they were swimming mistily.

"Sulky!" thought the Mayor in irritation.

He could not abide sulky people.

That silent, unhappy dinner was over at last and further disciplinary measures were postponed for the time being. The Mayor had a council meeting to attend and Marian made her escape to her room. Mrs. Carey would have to do the dishes without her help this one night.

But her grief was to be deferred a second time, for the telephone bell rang sharply and Mrs. Carey called that Lelia Mason wanted to speak to her.

"I could hardly wait till dinner was over," bubbled the unsuspecting Lelia. "Did he like it? What did he say?"

"He—he was cross!" Marian gulped. "He said I looked like a freak and he made me take off the dress and the beads and earrings, before we had dinner. And a barber has to cut my hair in the morning. I'll bring the things back to you to-morrow, Lelia. It wasn't your fault—I guess I can't look pretty, no matter how hard I try."

"You looked *nice,*" Lelia cried loyally. "Don't you care what your uncle said—he isn't a judge. Do you want me to save your hair?"

"Save my hair?" repeated Marian blankly.

"The braid, you know," Lelia explained. "Cousin Dora says it is a shame to throw away such a heavy braid—you could keep it; my mother has curls put away of my hair and my two brothers'."

"I haven't any mother to save it for," said the little voice at the other end of the wire desolately. "So—I guess you can throw it away, Lelia."

"I'm always saying something thoughtless like that," the warm-hearted Lelia cried, genuinely angry at herself. "Don't catch you doing a thing like that—you're a dear, Marian, and you never hurt anyone. Tell you what I'll do—take it home and sell it for you to a man who makes doll wigs and send you the money. Will that be all right?"

Marian expressed an odd twinge at the thought of her own hair being sold—it was really a part of herself, wasn't it?—but she certainly did not want to keep it, and some money would be very acceptable. She had none at all, except a single lucky penny that had been her father's "pocket piece."

So she said "all right," gratefully and hung up the receiver. To her surprise she didn't feel as much like crying as she had. She turned toward the kitchen.

"I'm almost finished—don't need you a mite," Mrs. Carey greeted her kindly. "Run on outdoors and see the yellow rose—there's one bud almost out."

Mrs. Carey felt sorry for the girl—she might look odd, she told herself as she dried the salad plates with care and precision, but it was only natural she had tried to "dress up."

"I think myself something light would become her more," said Mrs. Carey, apparently addressing the kitchen clock—she had a habit of talking aloud when alone—"but she has those dark things and they're perfectly good and almost new, if her aunt did make them out of her own dresses. Goodness knows I have enough to do without fussing over the fashions."

Marian slipped out into the garden and the warm, sweet June night folded her round like a cloak of healing. It seemed foolish to be unhappy in the face of that fragrant stillness. It was early dusk and Marian went quietly down the path to where the rose bushes were massed at the back of the house.

"Oh—o-h, Marian's had her hair cut!" a clear treble voice began the terrible chant on the other side of the hedge. "Marian's had her hair cut! Marian's had her hair cut!"

It was Dix, of course. His arm had healed with no complications and with little pain. While it had been bandaged, he had rather lorded it over Marian, finding it convenient and pleasant to have her read to him, bringing him sandwiches and lemonade at unexpected intervals and generally be at his beck and call. However, as soon as he could tag the other boys—which was when Doctor Armstrong removed the bandages and he no longer had to avoid contact with his injured member, Dix ungratefully forgot his neighbor and spent his days as usual, which meant tramping incessantly in an effort to keep up with his older brothers.

He had to endure many snubs and David as a rule would not tolerate his company. David was fond of going off by himself and he spent hours alone. Peter used to say that David was either a genius or too queer to be "right," but no comment could change David. Donald, Marian noted, was variable and sometimes he was fiercely tender and protective toward Dix, sometimes curt and overbearing in his assumption of authority.

"Marian's had her hair cut!" Dix continued to chant.

At different points along the hedge, heads began to rise. Donald was there, and David—Dix—the red-headed Cinnamon boy from the next block—Harold Jackson—another boy Marian did not know. To her horrified eyes, all the boys in the town seemed to be staring at her hair.

"What did you have it cut for?" demanded Donald.

"It looks like the dickens," the Cinnamon boy announced with beautiful frankness.

"Why don't you tie it back or something?"—this suggestion came from Harold Jackson and indeed Marian was constantly annoyed by straggling locks. Cut badly, the hair did not stay in place.

"It looked nicer before," said Dix and perhaps there is no criticism harder for the bobbed-haired one to endure than this.

"I don't say anything when you have your

hair cut," Marian pointed out, finding it difficult to address the unlooked for jury.

"That's different," said Donald. "I think you were awfully silly to get your hair bobbed. Peter said your hair was your one beauty."

"And now you haven't got that," Dix added unnecessarily.

"Then," said Marian demurely, "I certainly shall not be vain."

She stared over the hedge at him, a pathetic little figure with her untidy shorn head silhouetted against the fading light.

Dix stared back at her as solemnly. Marian looked queer.

And without warning she began to laugh. If her merriment was slightly hysterical and very close to tears, none of the youngsters staring over the hedge could sense that. One by one they followed her example and the gardens echoed to their laughter. When they looked for Marian again she had vanished and they soon forgot the episode. A girl's hair wasn't such an important matter.

CHAPTER X

WITH NEEDLE AND THREAD

MARIAN went to the barber on Main Street in the morning and he trimmed her hair into some semblance of order. All the time he worked he made little clicking noises with his tongue, symbolic of horror and astonishment. Lelia's tonsorial art was not such as to merit his approval.

The red beads and the earrings and the cerise dress were returned to their owner. Lelia reiterated her promise to take the braid of yellow hair to the doll wig maker. Her visit to her cousin ended in a few days and when she went away, Marian felt a new loneliness. Lelia had been gay and companionable and she had sought Marian out, partly because she, too, was a stranger in the rather clannish town. There were girls in Stillwell and undoubtedly in the fall, when the schools opened, Marian would have a fair chance to become acquainted with them.

It never entered the head of Mrs. Carey to ask any of the town girls to the house to meet

Marian—and they dubbed her "a nice little thing" and let it go at that. She lacked the mysterious something that draws friends as flowers do the bees and though Marian longed with all her heart for girl companions, she could not take the aggressive step. Mayor Bolton assumed that she must be happy as long as she did not ask him for anything and his housekeeper, glad that the newcomer was quiet by nature, had no desire to see her changed into a lively, harum-scarum creature dashing "hither and yon." A girl who didn't ask to be allowed to go anywhere was in Mrs. Carey's opinion as desirable as she was sensible.

The summer heat set in in earnest, with Lelia's departure and Peter Parsons' voice was raised in daily argument with Dix, who was so constituted that he could never shut a screen door unless reminded at least twice. Donald spent his days playing ball and the hottest part of the afternoon could be found, sunburned and dusty, captaining his "team" on a cross lot. Even Peter did not know what David did with his time —he was usually alone and, turning up at meal times, became cross and resentful if asked questions.

Dix alternately teased Marian or hung

around Peter's kitchen and annoyed him, unless he could follow the older boys. He would chase balls and lug the heavy water pail cheerfully for "the fellows," if they would let him. Peter used to scold when he came in at night, dead-tired and dripping wet from his exertions, but Dix was determined to be a ball player in a big league some day and he would not listen to any advice that tried to turn him from his ambition.

Marian saw a good deal of the household next door, for reticence was not a trait of the boys and Peter never lowered his voice when he had comment to make or reproof to bestow. He kept the house clean, if not neat, and he cooked wholesome meals, if sadly lacking in variety. But there were many details with which he made no attempt to cope and Marian marveled that no one stepped in to offer any help.

"My land, Marian, the Professor would chop my nose off if he caught me snooping around his house," Mrs. Carey said once, when Marian mentioned something of this.

"You can't go into a man's house and say, 'My dear sir, this place looks like all possessed; your boys are running wild and Dix has seven safety pins on his Galatea sailor suit—I counted them this morning.' If they were dreadful poor, or on the town, then a body could step in and straighten them out—not the way they are. I don't see how anyone could do a thing."

"But aren't they—poor?" asked Marian doubtfully.

"I don't suppose they're well off," Mrs. Carey admitted. "I never yet knew a university professor who was exactly rolling in wealth, unless he married it. And Professor Drayton married a girl without a cent to her name, but with a disposition that was worth a million; I've heard plenty of people say so. He has enough to live on, I suppose, and the house is free and clear. But it is so run down now, it will take a good deal of money to put it in shape. I believe he counts on sending the boys to college with the royalties he gets from his book. At the rate he is going, he may be able to finish it in time to send Dix."

Marian pondered over these conversations—she and Mrs. Carey had many a serious debate as they did the dinner dishes; the Mayor was usually off to some meeting, either in Stillwell or the city, or he might have appointments with important-looking men who came in soon after dinner and talked with him in the library.

"I don't believe Professor Drayton would chop off my nose," thought Marian. "I think it is—is—shocking for Dix to be going around pinned together like that. I'm going to tell Peter I know how to sew and mend."

And the next afternoon proved an auspicious time for her to make the announcement.

She had found a ragged dish towel on the grass on the Bolton side of the hedge and as Mrs. Carey had never been known to tolerate a ragged towel in her kitchen, it was safe to assume that a mischievous wind had blown it from the line in another yard—say the Drayton's.

Marian went through the gate and saw Peter on the back porch, bent intently over something. As he looked up and saw her, a dull red crept over his face.

"Just trying to sew up a hole," he explained, putting a basket behind him. "Guess I never was cut out to do fancy work."

"I wish you'd let me do it," said Marian earnestly. "I know how to darn and mend, Peter—I did it for my father. And Mrs. Carey keeps everything so spick and span at our house, there is never anything I can do to help her; she says if I sew, too, she won't have anything to do afternoons."

"She ought to have these three kids to look after," Peter growled. "The last girl the Professor got at the employment agency took the mending off my hands and I thought I was in for an easy time; but she only stayed three days and left the darning needle sticking in a sock of Dix's."

"What made her go?" asked Marian, forgetting the mending question for the moment.

"Donald put a garter snake in her bed, or some such business—maybe it was a pickle," Peter responded. "Either way, she had hysterics and left—I suppose I ought to see about getting someone else, or stir up the Professor to get a girl, but I hate to bother him; he's so good-natured about putting aside his work, you feel it's a sin to interrupt a man who only asks you to leave him alone. He'd eat bread and milk three times a day for a week and never complain, as long as he could write every day."

"Oh!" said Marian.

She picked up a blouse—Peter had his mending tumbled on a piece of newspaper spread on the porch floor.

"This sleeve is ripped—let me have a needle and thread," she commanded.

"This is the only needle I have," said Peter.

"Something's the matter with it, too—it will hardly go through this shirt."

He brought out the garment he had thrust behind him at Marian's approach and showed it to her.

"I thought it was about time the Professor had something done for him," declared Peter.

Marian never thought of smiling. She was as much concerned over the Drayton mending as Peter Parsons was. She never saw anything funny in the problems of her friends and while her sense of humor might not be very keen— as the Mayor complained—she had abundant tact and sympathy.

"Your thread is too large, that's all," Marian informed Peter, after inspecting his sewing. "That's the reason you can hardly drag the needle through—wait, I'll show you."

Peter had a pasteboard shoe box beside him and his meager equipment was in that. In a trice Marian had found a spool of the right size thread, had rethreaded the needle and was demonstrating that "sewing up a hole" could be easily accomplished by flexible fingers.

"I declare, I don't see how you do it," said Peter, stretching his cramped hands.

"Every finger I've got is sore from being

pricked. I never was cut out to do fancy work," he repeated.

"If you'll let me take these things home, I'll bring them back all fixed," Marian promised. "I won't say a word to Mrs. Carey, either, if you would rather I didn't. I have whole afternoons to myself and I'll sew up in my room where no one will ask me questions. You needn't be afraid that everyone in town will know I am sewing on buttons for the Draytons."

Peter looked at her in wordless admiration.

"You beat the Dutch!" he finally evolved. "Takes a mite of a girl like you to see right into things—I *would* hate to have the neighbors talking about the mending; goodness knows they have enough to talk about as it is and every once in so often they come calling to see how the housekeeping's going. The Professor never sees 'em, but I have to answer their questions and I know well enough they go home and say it's a wonder the family doesn't die of some disease, the way that Peter Parsons forgets to dust the square piano."

Marian laughed appreciatively.

"I won't gossip and I'll love to mend, every week," she said. "Who does the washing, Peter?"

"I do everything," proclaimed Peter proudly. "I found I could manage better alone. When we had a washerwoman, the tubs didn't suit her and she wanted an electric iron and the house isn't wired. Then we sent the wash out a couple of times but I missed some of the tablecloths, and anyway some of the clothes were so torn I didn't like to send 'em. It's better to do your washing home. I'm not saying it won't be a relief to have some buttons put on—Dix must eat 'em for he never has any on his clothes; but don't you think you ought to stay out in the open air, not be cooped up in a house sewing?"

"I can't stay out in the open air all the time," Marian said a little forlornly. "It will be nice to have something useful to do—Mrs. Carey hardly ever needs any help. I'll bring these back as soon as I have them fixed."

She departed triumphantly with the newspaper bundle under her arm and that was the beginning of a mending service that for reliability, promptness and thoroughness, could not have been duplicated anywhere within the borough. Marian was a skillful little needlewoman for her age and exquisitely painstaking. She could patch and darn and sew on buttons in a way to defeat even the strenuous efforts of the active Dix. She was mindful of her promise, too, and never said a word to anyone of the work she did. As long as she was apparently happy and occupied, neither the Mayor nor Mrs. Carey questioned her as to how she spent her time. The Mayor had outlined a few rules for his housekeeper's guidance the first week Marian came—she was not to "run the streets"; she was not to leave the house after dinner without asking permission and if she had any "unusual plans," he was to be consulted before they were carried out.

"There never was a child, less like her mother, than Marian," said Mrs. Carey to her confidante, the faithful Miss Palmer. "Her looks and her disposition favor her Aunt Amelia—I've said it from the first and I'll say it a hundred times. Unusual plans indeed—Marian never had a plan in her head, I'll be bound."

Which only showed that Mrs. Carey, too, had in mind the "plans" of Nancy Bolton, whose dashing ideas were apt to involve the entire younger element of Stillwell.

Marian was happier, after she had her sewing, because it furnished her with occupation for her hands. She read a great deal and was allowed perfect freedom in her uncle's fine library—but no active girl can read all day long. When, one morning after the Mayor had left as usual to get his train, Mrs. Carey sank, white-faced into a kitchen chair and owned to a blinding sick headache, Marian really welcomed the opportunity to be of actual service.

"I'll put you to bed," she said capably, "and then I'll tend to things—shall I ask Doctor Armstrong to come and see you?"

"Mercy no," groaned the sufferer. "I'll be all right by night—if I'm not, you'll have to get Effie to come in and cook dinner."

And she went on murmuring her plans for salad, and regretting that she had not made a fresh cake the day before, until Marian, as nurse, felt she must insist her patient allow herself to be put to bed.

CHAPTER XI

THE DREAM HOUSE

MRS. CAREY was subject to these headaches and hitherto she had taken care of herself as best she could, spending the day in bed and struggling up, if possible, to cook the dinner at night. If, as sometimes happened, five o'clock still found her in that unhappy state of not being able to "raise her head from the pillow," she would send one of the Drayton boys for the faithful Effie. Though the skies fell, as Effie remarked, Mayor Bolton must find his dinner waiting for him at the usual time.

It was distinctly novel, and quite as restful, for Mrs. Carey to find herself taken in charge this morning. Marian coaxed her to lie down on her bed, took off her shoes and covered her lightly. Then she sponged the patient's face and hands with toilet water and drew the shades. As if by magic the room became an airy, shady place, a faint fragrance seemed to hover in the cool air and Mrs. Carey felt her eyelids beginning to droop.

"I didn't sleep much last night," she confessed. "I tried to do too much yesterday. Now don't bother with anything downstairs, Marian—I'll be all right as soon as I have had a nap."

"Yes'm," said Marian sedately.

She closed the bedroom door softly and went down to the kitchen. In swift and orderly succession she washed and dried the breakfast dishes, put the kitchen to rights, dusted the living room and swept off the front and side porches. The grocery boy came with the order given the day before and Marian found the right place for each article with little trouble. She hummed happily as she worked and twice glanced in at Mrs. Carey, who was sleeping peacefully.

Noon found her still sleeping and Marian enjoyed a solitary lunch on the kitchen table. It was fun to choose what she liked from the ice box and she decided that when she had a house of her own she would have a picnic lunch every day. She was glad the neighborhood was so still—no noise from next door to penetrate the rest of poor Mrs. Carey. Marian remembered seeing the three Drayton boys starting out soon after breakfast—that explained the quiet. They would probably be gone till dinner time and that meant an untroubled afternoon.

At two o'clock Marian peeped into Mrs. Carey's room again and saw that she was awake.

"Could you drink a cup of tea?" she asked her patient hopefully.

Mrs. Carey blinked and felt gingerly of her aching head.

"I don't know but I could," she said. "Maybe I could get up if I had something hot to drink first."

Marian made the tea and toasted two thin slices of bread. She arranged this daintily on a small tray and carried it upstairs.

"My land, you might think I was the Queen of England!" exclaimed Mrs. Carey. "I never was one to be waited upon. I guess after this I can make ice cream for dinner to-night."

But when she had eaten the toast and disposed of the tea, she complained of feeling dizzy.

"I'd be all right if I didn't have to hold my head up," she explained a trifle fretfully, being one of those people who enjoy such excellent health as a rule that the slightest illness rouses their impatience.

"What you need is to stay in bed and keep perfectly still," said Marian.

"I'll go and get Effie—she'll know how to do everything and you won't need to worry at all. Lie down and sleep some more and by tomorrow morning you'll be as good as new"—she smiled so confidently that the housekeeper, whose usually well-behaved head was performing in an alarming manner, sank back on her cool pillows almost contentedly.

"I declare you're a sight of comfort, Marian," she said gratefully. "You know where Effie lives? Down by the railroad—tell her to come early and that I want her to stay and do the dishes, too. And there's everything ready, because I put in my order yesterday."

"I'll tell her," Marian promised. "Everything will be all right—you'll see. Just you lie down and try to doze."

She took away the tray and went down to the kitchen.

"Now Daddy would know I could get dinner," she said to herself, a little wistfully.

"I could get a nice dinner, not fancy, but really good to eat; only perhaps Uncle Cornelius wouldn't be satisfied—Effie will be better. I'd better go and tell her right away—I wonder if she is always home?"

Marian's start was delayed, however, unexpectedly. As she went down the drive, a paper fluttered over the hedge and fell almost at her feet. She picked it up and gazed around inquiringly. Upstairs in the Drayton house, the Professor was signaling violently.

"I'll come down and get it," he called.

Marian, eager to save him steps, ran across the lawn and met him at the front door.

"It's some of my notes," Professor Drayton explained. "A tricky breeze played havoc with the papers on my table."

He rubbed his hair with a gesture of perplexity.

"I'm afraid I don't follow the instructions I used to give my students," he said ruefully.

"I seldom can put my hands on the notes I need. Worse still, I write an abominable hand and I am not always able to decipher my own writing without study. Of course I waste much valuable time sorting out notes that should be in sequence from the first writing."

His tired eyes rested on the sun-soaked street and brightened.

"I didn't realize it was such a pleasant day,"

he said, speaking more to himself than to the little figure before him.

"Why, it is a beautiful day!" cried Marian, surprised. "I just love summer—don't you? And Stillwell is so pretty—I never saw so many trees."

"Yes, it is pleasant, very pleasant," the Professor admitted.

"Well, I must go back to my work—thank you for rescuing the paper, child."

He smiled at her and she was oddly reminded of Dix and his engaging grin. As she went down the street, bounded for Effie's, Marian wondered if she could not do something about the Professor's notes.

"Daddy used to say I was neat," she thought, "and of course I could number pages and arrange them in the right order. Perhaps I could read Professor Drayton's notes, too—I like to puzzle things out."

She was no longer on Euclid Avenue, but on one of the cross streets the name of which she did not remember noticing. Absorbed in her growing plan to help the Professor, she paid little heed to her surroundings and when someone spoke—apparently to her—Marian frankly jumped.

"My dear child, will you do something for me?" a voice asked.

It was a beautiful voice, rich and sweet and peculiarly distinct. Marian looked around, but could see no one. She had halted on a concrete walk—noticeable because in Stillwell the majority of walks were the flagstones, more picturesque than uniformly even—and she now saw that she stood before a brick house built flush with the pavement. On either side of the house was a high iron fence through which could be seen a glimpse of brilliant gardens apparently endless in extent.

"Look up—look up!" urged the voice, a hint of amusement in the charming cadence now.

Obediently Marian raised her glance to the casement windows in the second story of the brick house. Was there someone there?

"I dropped something out of the window," the unseen speaker continued. "Oh, not there" as Marian involuntarily looked around her. "I dropped it on the grass, from one of the side windows. I wonder if you would get it and bring it to me?"

"Why—why, of course!" stammered Marian, slightly bewildered.

"I'll throw down the key to you," the voice

announced. "Unlock the gate on the right and be sure to latch it after you. I'll let you in."

A silver tinkle sounded at Marian's feet and she saw the key which had been dropped. She was rather glad that it was the hour when all Stillwell napped or at least stayed quietly indoors—there was no one to see her as she struggled to fit the key in the lock of the iron gate. It did not fit in easily and she guessed that the lock was not often used. However, once she had the key in and turned, the gate swung lightly open. Mindful of instructions, she closed it after her and felt, as she heard the little click, almost like a prisoner.

"She didn't say what she had dropped," she thought, wondering what she was to pick up.

But just ahead of her she saw it—something white and fluffy that, on examination, proved to be a little sweater in the process of knitting. The ball of yarn was with it and the needles.

Marian retrieved the sweater and looked for an entrance to the house. She did not recall having seen a door on the street side, but then she had not looked very carefully at the house itself. Here, however, was a little jewel of a doorway, set in the red brick, between two wide windows and painted a spotless, shining white.

The door swung noiselessly open as Marian approached it and closed behind her without a sound. She was standing in a room that was evidently the width of the house, a room with dark wood work and gleaming polished floors and furnished in startling contrast. Chairs, tables and even the small grand piano were ivory white and white goatskin rugs were spread on the shining floor.

The lady who came forward to greet her was in white, too—soft lacey white that broke into foamy ruffles at her throat and wrists and again above the hem of her frock. Her shoes were white and so were the masses of her hair and alas, the lovely face was white, too, with a paleness that made the dark eyes look unnaturally large and bright. No wonder Marian stared— she had never seen anyone like this.

"Thank you so much, my dear," said the lady in the same rich voice Marian had heard from the window.

She took the sweater and the gate key from the girl's hands and motioned toward a chair.

"I—I can't stay," Marian declared, quite sure in her own mind that she was dreaming and would presently wake up in her own bed.

"I have to go and get Effie to come and cook dinner."

"Well, dinner is undoubtedly of importance," conceded the lady in white, "but I hoped you could stay and talk to me a little. I know you do not live in Stillwell—that is why I called to you."

"But I do—I do live here," Marian protested. "I'm Marian Blessing, and I live with my Uncle Cornelius."

"There is no family named Blessing in Stillwell," said the lady in white with a gentle obstinacy.

"I live with Mayor Bolton—he's my uncle and I think my guardian, since Daddy died." Marian explained diffidently, for she was not sure in her own mind whether her uncle was really her guardian.

"I know of the Mayor," said the lady, but she did not mention Nancy Bolton, though most people instantly connected his name with that of his brilliant half sister's.

"I'll have to go and get Effie," Marian said again, uneasily.

"Will you come in and see me—another day?" the lady urged. "I should like to know you. And I never leave the house—that is why I asked you to pick up the sweater for me; I dropped it from the window seat upstairs."

Marian promised to come again and the lady pressed a button set in the wall. The door swung open silently and Marian found herself in the garden.

There was a catch on the inside of the gate, she discovered, and by pressing this, the lock was released and the gate could be opened.

"It must have been a dream," said Marian dazedly, as she continued her walk. "It didn't really happen at all."

Then the old test came to her mind.

"I'll pinch myself," she said determinedly. "If I am asleep, it won't hurt—ouch!"

For her pinch had been sufficiently vigorous to be painful, and proved beyond the shadow of a doubt that she was wide awake.

Still I feel different," Marian mused, loth to leave the unexplainable as she had found it.

"I feel a great deal different," she assured herself, bewildered.

CHAPTER XII

LELIA'S LETTER

"YOU sure you feel all right, Miss Marian?" asked Effie with real concern in her friendly tone.

"You look a little mite peaked to me," the good-natured girl went on. "Like as not, you did too much this morning, trying to take care of Mis' Carey."

"No, I'm all right," Marian returned absently, stroking the yellow kitten which had leaped into her lap.

The houses near the railroad were small, and huddled together too closely for beauty or even quiet comfort. The yards knew flexible boundary lines and seemed linked together by endless lengths of clothes lines on which discouraged-looking, faded garments were perpetually flapping. Sunflowers were practically the only form of horticulture that could be said to flourish in this environment and they shot up cheerfully in the most neglected corners.

The smaller the houses, the more dogs and cats, Marian had thought as she walked slowly, trying to pick out the house that looked like Effie's. She had a well-defined idea as to the appearance of Effie's house—it would be neat and gay, a little different from the others, she was sure. Effie loved color and Mrs. Carey used to say that she could see her coming to work when she was four blocks away—but then Mrs. Carey confined her color schemes to black and brown and gray and was perhaps a trifle intolerant of gaudier tastes.

Marian's reasoning proved correct—when she came to a house painted a deep, deep yellow, with turkey red curtains fluttering against the "homemade" screens neatly covered with white cotton netting, and a double row of sunflowers from the rickety gate to the front door, sure enough there was Effie hanging up something in the yard.

It was the fashion to hang one's wash in the front yard, in this section, partly because the railroad cut through the rear yards and in some cases did away with them altogether, and partly because there was more to see on the street. The housewives did not feel that they should deprive themselves of whatever amusement or instruction was available, merely because of the press of domestic duties. In their method of combining work with pleasure, there was a lesson in philosophy which might have been followed with profit by the ladies who kept house on the other side of town and who were frequently martyrs to their sense of devotion and duty.

"Sure I'll come round and cook dinner for you-all," said Effie, when Marian had stated her errand. "I'll be there quarter of five, sharp. You tell Mis' Carey not to give another thought —I'll get the Mayor a bang-up dinner and do the dishes and everything afterward. There aren't any movies to-night."

Effie was a motion-picture fan and never failed to stipulate that she was to be free to attend the "first run" of the new pictures. The program was changed only three times a week at the one theater in town and on the nights when new pictures were shown it was useless to expect Effie to wash any dishes—that was in her contract.

Marian walked home, puzzling over the mystery of the brick house and the lady in white. One thing was certain—she was not going to ask any questions.

"It's like a fairy story—she's an enchanted princess and she lives in a secret tower," thought Marian, her imagination kindling.

"Perhaps she is shut away from her enemies and perhaps she is hiding from a wicked witch. Donald and the boys have their secrets and never tell me a thing—I'm going to have this for my secret."

Though she would not have admitted it, Marian was often hurt by the careless attitude of the Drayton lads. David could not be called friendly, so she expected little from him, but Donald and Dix had moments when they were apparently ready to admit her to their councils and to treat her, if not as an equal, at least as a human being. She learned to use the flying rings in the barn, to walk on top of a fence rail without squealing and to play "catch" for an hour at a time with the sun in her eyes. Dix no longer went around looking like an advertisement for a brand of safety pins, but as the method by which his clothing was held together interested him very little, so long as the results passed muster, it is doubtful if he realized any change. Certainly he did not know that Marian was responsible. Peter Parsons was voluble in his thanks and he was always sure that Marian would tire of her self-imposed task "the next week." It had been his experience with the boys that whatever they undertook they wearied of it after slight repetition. He was agreeably surprised at the perseverance of his youthful neighbor.

But if Donald and Dix had moments when they were gracious and friendly, they had days when they ignored her altogether or, what was worse, teased her unmercifully and made her the object of their practical jokes. Donald was quick and clever and rather disposed to disparage anyone whose mental processes were slower than his—he quite openly said that Marian was "stupid" when she failed to grasp his meaning at the first involved sentence and he criticized her incessantly, which merely had the effect of making her self-conscious. Another type of girl would have "flared up," but Marian's even, placid manner was not to be ruffled on the surface. She took her loneliness as something to be accepted and gradually, almost imperceptibly, began to fill in her time with small plans and interests of her own. But anything as lovely and as satisfying as a princess in a secret tower had not occurred to her—no wonder she was unwilling to share this delight with the merely curious.

Mrs. Carey's head was better—much better the invalid declared—when Marian looked in to report that Effie would be on hand to get the dinner, but she was easily persuaded to lie quietly and not attempt to even sit up. She wanted nothing for dinner, she directed, but a cup of clear soup.

Marian went on to her own room to change her frock. She would have liked to dress in white, remembering the picture the lady in the brick house had made, but she had no white shoes and, for that matter, no white dress. She compromised on a print that had a white background and a small dark blue figure. She found herself wishing that her hair had not been bobbed, though there was no gainsaying its convenience. She brushed the shining yellow strands now, guiltless of a wave, but trimly cut to show the outlines of her well-shaped head.

The bell rang as she tied the laces in her serviceable best shoes and she ran down to admit Effie, who charged upon the kitchen as a general upon his campaign plans. Marian knew there was nothing she could do to help, so she sat down comfortably in the porch swing and was still there when the Mayor's car rolled up the drive: he had come out earlier than usual.

"Hello," he greeted her, "you look cool and serene. I found a letter for you in the box."

He sat down opposite her and left the car standing—that meant he was going out after dinner.

"A letter for me?" asked Marian, pleasantly excited.

"A letter for you," her uncle smiled. "The afternoon mail was just sorted as I passed the post-office."

He handed her a square white envelope and unfolded his newspaper. Marian had hoped he might go in, as he usually did, to get ready for dinner, but evidently he intended to rest a few minutes on the porch.

The letter was from Lelia Mason—Marian knew from the postmark—and as she opened it, a slip of green paper fluttered out and slid across the floor.

The Mayor captured the slip and looked surprised when he saw what it was. Marian supposed it was a check and she felt that some explanation would be expected.

"It's a check," she said, "from Lelia."

"A money order," the Mayor corrected.

"Oh, is it?" Marian stared at the green slip in open perplexity. "I suppose it is for my hair," she murmured.

"For your hair?" repeated her astonished uncle.

"Lelia was going to sell it," Marian said. "To a man who makes wigs for dolls."

Mayor Bolton stared at the smooth head against the cretonne pillow and then he began to understand.

"You mean your hair that was cut off," he declared. "Lelia seems to be a resourceful girl."

Marian scanned the letter—she would read it more carefully another time—and as she folded it to replace it in the envelope, her uncle held out his hand. Mechanically she gave him the missive—she had received and sent so few letters in her thirteen years that there had been no occasion for any supervision of her correspondence.

Mayor Bolton read the letter through and handed it back without making any comment. But his first words were a surprise to his niece.

"I think you ought to have a regular weekly allowance, Marian," he said quietly. "I've thought of it several times, but so many things have been taking my time—these pesky special meetings—"

He broke off and stared across the lawn for a few moments in silence.

"Not that a girl living at home has any definite expenditures," he went on presently. "Er—what do you plan to do with this money order, for instance?"

"Buy a white dress!" his niece assured him instantly.

The Mayor laughed and Marian discovered that his keen eyes could twinkle pleasantly.

"You do know what you want, don't you?" he said. "I thought Mrs. Carey was looking after the clothes problem for you."

"She does—she is," cried Marian, anxious that the housekeeper should not be criticized, even by implication, "but, you see, Uncle Cornelius, I want a white dress and Mrs. Carey would think I didn't need it. I have plenty of dresses, but they're all made the same way and they are all dark and ugly."

"I don't know anything about it," the Mayor said, stuffing his paper in his pocket and rising to go in, "but if you say you want a white dress, I don't doubt that you do. And every Saturday morning I'll see that you get a small sum of spending money—not a great deal, for I don't approve of boys and girls having much money until they have learned to make expenditures wisely."

Marian stayed quietly in the swing. She was planning what she would do with her allowance. She meant to save it carefully and when she had enough she would go shopping. She had studied Lelia and Lelia's clothes and she knew that pretty dresses helped to make pretty girls prettier and even plain girls more attractive. She would not make the mistake of getting a red frock, but there were other colors.

Effie served an excellent dinner, but it was Marian who carried the soup up to Mrs. Carey and promised to come back and make her comfortable for the night. She was taking the empty cup back to the kitchen when a low whistle startled her.

"Say, Marian, I'm starving," whispered Dix, his nose flattened against the screen door of the pantry through which she had to pass to reach the kitchen—"I wish you'd sneak me something to eat—will you, Marian? Is there any pie?"

Marian regarded him with well-founded suspicion.

"Why aren't you home, eating your own dinner?" she demanded.

"Aw, Pete's mad because I was a little late and we had an argument," came the explanation from Dix.

CHAPTER XIII

ANOTHER JOB

DIX and Peter, in the course of their relationship had numerous arguments. Peter's discipline was extremely spasmodic and poor Dix sometimes complained, with justice, that he was held accountable for misdeeds which had previously drawn forth no word or sign of disapproval.

As he ate the food Marian hastily assembled on a plate and brought out to him, he explained that "Pete" had for a week been threatening the boys with no dinner, unless they returned at the hour he specified.

"He wants us to eat at half past five," grumbled Dix, between mouthfuls. "Dad doesn't mind because he likes to write all he can before you have to light the gas, but it's fierce to have to come home before any of the other fellows do. Pete says he isn't going to work all day and all night, too—he wants some time to sit out on the porch, after the supper dishes are done."

"I should think he would," Marian said. "Were you late to-night?"

"Kind of," admitted Dix, stuffing a whole corn fritter into his mouth by the simple expedient of rolling it up like a cylinder.

"What did Donald and David do for some dinner?" asked Marian, considerately waiting till the fritter had been safely swallowed.

"They have things out in the barn," Dix said. "Potted ham and canned fruit and things; but they won't ever let me have any. We were only a little late—we got home quarter of seven," he added, returning to his main grievance. "An' Pete had everything put away and wouldn't let us in the kitchen. Dad was writing, upstairs, or he would have let us cook eggs or something."

Marian rescued the now empty plate which was in danger of sliding down the porch steps.

"I think Peter did perfectly right," she said mildly. "If you had ever cooked a dinner, Dix, you'd know that you cannot keep it hot from half past five till quarter of seven."

"Didn't want it hot," the unrepentant Dix retorted. "Just wanted something to eat."

He slid off the steps and vanished into the shrubbery, probably intent on making an attempt to raid the older boy's cache. Dix was optimistic by nature and not at all adverse to trying the same thing any number of times.

Marian heard Peter's version of the episode next morning, when she went over to see about the weekly mending. She liked to sew and her father had always encouraged her efforts and praised her lavishly, so that it had been no hardship to use her little work-basket regularly. Now she was thankful for the self-training, for it made it easier for her to be faithful to the endless call for buttons, the chronic ailment from which every garment in the Drayton household seemed to suffer.

"I have to draw the line somewhere," said Peter, who was in the garden, picking the last of the peas.

"Those kids are getting so they don't mind a word I say, but there's one way of arguing with a boy that, to my thinking, hasn't any comparison; cut down on his food and you have him just where you want him."

Marian's conscience gave a feeble twinge. She had not supported Peter in his attempt to put his theory into practice.

"I said 'no dinner' last night to those boys and I'll bet you a cookie they turn up to-night right on the dot," Peter went on, happily unaware of her thoughts.

"An hour and a half past the time is a little too much— I guess Job would have been vexed, if he had to put up with what I have to stand."

"It's easier for some people to be punctual than it is for others," Marian reminded him, watching the peas fall into the basket as he picked with quick nervous jerks of his toil-stained fingers.

"Why doesn't their father speak to them?" she added.

"The Professor? Bless you, he wouldn't ever come down to eat unless I went up myself and fetched him—" Peter's tone was affectionately indulgent.

"He's feeling mean to-day—got one of his headaches. He needs new glasses, but every time he goes into the city to get fitted, he doesn't get any nearer the eyeglass place than the Public Library."

"Mrs. Carey had a headache yesterday, but she's all right now," volunteered Marian. "You ought to give him tea and toast."

"He won't go to bed—sits up there trying to read his notes and him half blind from the pain," Peter answered. "That book will be the end of him yet if he doesn't put it aside now and then."

"I wish I could copy those notes," said Marian impulsively. "I could number the pages and put them in order—I do believe I'll go up now and ask him."

She had chosen an excellent time to approach the Professor on her suggestion. He was seated at his desk, the windows all down to prevent a repetition of the accident of the day before and the heat was stifling. He had left the door open into the hall and Marian caught a glimpse of him, his head resting on his hand, before she knocked.

"Well, Marian," he greeted her with an attempt at cheerfulness, "you didn't find any more of my papers blowing about the lawn, did you?"

"Not to-day," Marian replied, "but Mr. Drayton, I wish you'd let me sort your notes out for you and number the pages; if any need recopying, I can do that, too. I know how valuable they are and I'll be so careful not to lose a single sheet."

"I couldn't think of letting you do that," said the Professor quickly. "No young girl should be expected to do heavy clerical work in this kind of weather. Your uncle would be highly displeased and he would have every reason to be."

Marian sat down on one of the chairs with a smaller pile of books on it than the rest.

"It isn't heavy work," she argued in her pleasant voice. "I like to put things in order. I kept a card index file for Daddy, and he said my handwriting was clear and easy to read."

"But I need my notes almost constantly," said the Professor, looking around at the mass of papers as though he wasn't sure he could find what he needed at short notice.

"After I once had them arranged it would be easy to keep them that way," Marian pointed out. "Peter said you have a headache, so you probably won't work to-day, anyway; if you'll let me take the notes over and work on them now, I think I could promise to bring them back in the morning."

Professor Drayton was sorely tempted. He had reached the point in his work where it was imperative that he have access to his notes with the least possible delay. Between the breezes which swept the room unmolested when Peter insisted on putting up the windows to "air the place," and Peter's own well-meant but devastating efforts to "regulate" the desk in the brief absences of the owner, the papers were in a sad whirl and he had that morning spent an unprofitable hour searching for several brilliant paragraphs he now feared were lost forever.

"It's an imposition," he hesitated. "What will your uncle say?"

"Uncle Cornelius won't mind," said Marian confidently. "He likes me to be busy—and I'm not allowed to go anywhere after dinner, so this will be lovely work. I do read and sew," she hurried on, defensively, "but a day is a pretty long stretch when there isn't anyone to play with."

This little speech would have revealed to a discerning person that the speaker knew what it meant to be lonely. However, wise and kind as he was, Professor Frederick Drayton was not given to analyzing spoken words. He would devote months to accurately defining an obscure root and its derivatives and branches, but the hidden meaning in commonplace English seldom attracted his attention.

"You are very good," he said, rather formally. "I will confess that the help you suggest will be of inestimable value to me. But you are not to hurry—there must be no overtaxing of your mental or physical forces. I will employ myself on the preface, while you are arranging the notes. Promise me you will not work at them too steadily."

"I'll be reasonable," Marian smiled, beginning to gather up the yellow and white papers which strewed the desk and couch.

"And you will lie down, won't you?" she begged him with pretty anxiety. "Mrs. Carey cured her headache just by staying in bed."

"I do believe I will rest my eyes—for a day," said the Professor, rubbing his forehead wearily. "Peter is after me to get new glasses—be thankful for your good vision, Marian, and don't risk it by studying or reading at night."

He helped her gather up the papers into a large, untidy bundle and she went gleefully downstairs, stopping on the back porch to tell Peter Parsons of the success of her mission.

"You don't want to start in and bring up Dix, do you?" he asked her humorously. "You seem to be helping us out where we need it most—though when it comes to that, Dave is the one that needs attention. I can still spank Dix when it comes right down to it, but Dave is beyond me."

"David hardly ever has a word to say to me," said Marian slowly.

"He hardly ever has a word for anyone," Peter

retorted. "If ever there was a close-mouthed lad, it's Dave Drayton. Goes around as glum as an owl—never cares much what the other boys are doing, as long as they let him alone. He has a hot temper, too, and when he's aroused they get from under. It's a funny thing, but his father can do more with Dave than anyone else —I do believe Dave thinks more of the Professor than the other two do. Not that he shows it— he doesn't show anything he can help."

Marian shifted the sheaf of note papers to the other arm and bent down to pick up the bundle of mending.

"How long have you lived here, Peter?" she asked, conscious of a real respect and liking for the grizzle-haired lame man who was so devoted to this odd family.

"I've been here since Dix was born," Peter answered proudly. "I remember that day well. Mrs. Drayton died when he was about a year old and after that the Professor lost interest in everything except his book. His wife was a pretty little woman and a born manager—kept everything as neat as a pin, including her three babies. She had a cook and a nurse and I was handy man and did the garden work. I've practically brought up Dix, because we couldn't keep a nurse for him after his mother died—the other two boys were too much for 'em. Yes, Dix is my baby and he's a fine chap, barring a little mischief, now and then."

"Dix is a dear," said Marian warmly, "and I like Donald and David, too. Isn't it funny, they all have the same initials—'D. D.'"

"Yes, it sounds funny," Peter admitted cautiously, "but that was partly the reason the servants struck; the boys were forever claiming each other's clothes and marking 'em with initials only made it worse. Then they developed a trick of carving up the furniture and they carved their initials on the bannisters and such places and you couldn't tell which one did it. It got so every time I saw 'D. D.' on a chair leg or the bannister rail, I'd spank Donald and David and put them to bed without supper, just on general principles. I figured Dix was too small to be handling a knife in those days."

"You must have done so much for them!"—Marian spoke impulsively.

"I mean looking after them and trying to run the house, too. Wasn't there ever anyone to help you?"

"There was an aunt," admitted Peter reflectively. "Seems to me she was a great-aunt, or a step-aunt—anyway, she wasn't an out-and-out relation. She came a month or two after Mrs. Drayton died, and she wanted the boys to wear mourning. She left when I wouldn't put a black tie on David's white blouse."

"Bringing up children is certainly hard work," said Marian seriously. "I imagine boys are worse than girls."

"I've heard it said they are more lively," Peter returned, "but no boy could think of more things to do than your mother could—Mrs. Drayton, you know, was her particular friend and I've heard about her pranks. They still talk at the University about what Miss Bolton did and said."

"Did you ever see my mother?" asked Marian eagerly.

"No-o I never did—she had married and gone away from Stillwell before my time," Peter said regretfully. "But Mrs. Drayton always said she was the most beautiful girl she ever knew and the pictures she had made it seem as if it must be so. It's funny she should have been so dark and you just the opposite."

CHAPTER XIV

THE BOROUGH COUNSEL

PUTTING the Professor's notes into any semblance of order proved a decidedly more difficult task than Marian had anticipated. He wrote with pencil or pen, whichever happened to be handier, and some of the words were so blurred as to be almost indecipherable. Then, too, he had a "shorthand" system of his own and because of the novel abbreviations, it was often necessary to read entire paragraphs to get at his meaning. Marian spent the greater part of the day numbering pages and copying portions of the notes which, because of the soft lead pencil affected by the Professor, threatened to become altogether lost.

By dinner time she had completed perhaps a third of the work.

At the dinner table that night her uncle surprised her with one of his rare questions.

"Have you been out to-day, Marian?" he asked, glancing at her rather keenly.

"I—oh, yes, this morning—I went over to the

Draytons'," Marian floundered self-consciously.

"Not a long walk, from the view point of exercise," said the Mayor, smiling. "I want you to stay out doors at least several hours a day; summer is the one season when this should not be an unpleasant stipulation. I trust you to remember it."

"Yes, sir," Marian murmured.

"I'm going to run out and see Singleton this evening," went on Mayor Bolton—"he lives near town and it isn't a long drive. Perhaps you'd like to go along?"

He so seldom asked her to drive with him that the invitation really startled her, but she managed to stammer an acceptance. It would be delicious to relax in the silent, high-powered car and the notes, on which she had planned to spend the evening till bedtime, could wait.

Mr. Singleton was the Borough Counsel and, like most of the prominent citizens of Stillwell, was also well known in the city where he had a large law practice. He lived a few miles from the center of the town, but still within the borough limits, on a large estate, beautifully kept and scientifically farmed. Marian was glad to be left in the car, under the sweep of the portecochère, while her uncle went in to see the lawyer.

The great white pillars of the porch were exquisitely spaced and the bricked floor of the porch was strewn with luxurious rugs and gayly cushioned wicker furniture. In the gathering dusk on the lawn, fireflies were beginning to dance and the newest of new crescent moons suddenly showed in the bit of sky between two graceful elm trees.

"It's lovely," ran the thoughts of the girl sitting so quietly in the car. "I wonder if Mr. Singleton likes it—but of course, he does. I think to-morrow I'll get Lelia's money-order cashed and buy the material for my white dress. I can make it if Mrs. Carey will show me what to do when it is time to put in the sleeves."

She was busily sewing on lace ruffles, when the sound of voices aroused her from her dreaming. Mr. Singleton had accompanied his guest to the door and now, perceiving that his car was parked at the side steps, he switched on the lights, scarcely needed, and peered a little curiously at the slight figure, almost lost in the heavy upholstery.

"My niece, Marian Blessing," said the Mayor perfunctorily, his mind evidently still on a previous conversation.

"Well, well, I did hear you had a niece coming

to live with you," Mr. Singleton rumbled in the deepest voice Marian had ever heard. "Makes it cheerful for you, eh, Bolton? My family's in Europe," he added, smiling at Marian, "and I tell you I miss my daughters when they are not around to keep me in order."

Marian smiled shyly. She liked this big man, who in some way seemed to match his house so satisfactorily. The lawyer was tall and broad-shouldered and though his hair was white—he had a habit of ruffling it till every lock stood on end—his dark eyes were alive and vigorous.

"We're no nearer a solution than we were six months ago, then," said the Mayor, taking his place behind the wheel.

"No nearer," Mr. Singleton agreed in his rumbling voice. "No nearer—but something may turn up at the Council meeting next week. You cannot force these issues, Bolton."

The Mayor grunted something that was unintelligible and started the car. As they rolled smoothly out of the driveway, Marian glanced back. Mr. Singleton still stood on the steps and he waved his hand genially.

"What a beautiful place!" Marian exclaimed involuntarily.

"Yes, Singleton is proud of it and has reason

to be," her uncle answered, the frown of concentration still between his eyes.

"He's several times a millionaire and I don't believe his farming has ever paid him a cent; but he has the show place of the neighborhood and cattle experts from all states in the Union come to study his registered herds."

Marian would have liked to hear more, but the Mayor lapsed into his usual taciturn silence. It was nearly nine o'clock when they reached the house and though they found Professor Drayton sitting on the porch, awaiting them, Marian merely greeted him and went on to her room. She knew that she was expected to go to bed at nine o'clock and it was difficult to do otherwise than she was expected to do in the household of Mayor Bolton. The Drayton lads might successfully outwit their good-natured, absent-minded father, or wear down the resistance of Peter Parsons, and make their bed hour an elastic thing, but Marian was sure that few people pitted their wills against the Mayor's and were victorious. Certainly not in a matter connected with his domestic schedule.

Marian thought Professor Drayton would mention the notes and so was not surprised the next morning when the Mayor brought up the subject at the breakfast table.

"Professor Drayton tells me that you have very kindly offered to try and put his notes in order for him," said the Mayor, selecting a perfectly browned piece of toast from Mrs. Carey's generous offering.

"I have no objections," he went on, speaking as he invariably did to Marian as though he were addressing someone of his own age, "if you will remember that you are to get sufficient exercise in the open air every day. Where are you doing these notes?"

"Upstairs—in my room," said his niece.

"Have you a desk or a flat-topped table?"

"No-o, I sit on the floor," Marian confessed.

"Then I'd recommend that you use the library table—not my desk—I cannot have my desk touched," said the Mayor as though he already foresaw an advancing army. "But the table is large and well placed between the windows and you can work there undisturbed. I'm glad you have undertaken this work if you can really lend the Professor a hand; he's so proud it's next to impossible to get him to accept any kind of assistance and yet I feel that his house must be a bedlam. I don't believe he knows what is going on around him half the time."

Marian wondered what he would say—or for that matter, the Professor—if he knew of the mending she had undertaken. However, that was her secret and if the Professor's conscience had impelled him to inform the Mayor that his niece was helping him with his literary work, no such motive troubled the head of the little niece. She was glad to have the library table placed at her disposal—there were obvious drawbacks to working on the floor. Mrs. Carey never went near the library, except to dust and clean it, and the Mayor was in the city all day. Marian knew she could work undisturbed and when the notes weighed too heavily on her, she had only to stretch out her hand to find a book ready to rest her tired mind.

But this morning she had important things on hand. She wished to cash the money order and buy the material for the white dress. It was a cool morning, too, just the kind of a day to go "uptown."

"Run along and have a good time, dearie," said Mrs. Carey, who sensed vaguely that something was lacking in the daily life of this girl though, had her own life been at stake, she could not have named what was missing.

"Run along and have a good time. Buy yourself a soda—I have some change—" and she began to fumble in her worn black pocketbook.

"Oh, I have loads of money," said Marian with the recklessness of a person whose weekly allowance is still untouched. "Uncle Cornelius is lovely about spending money—I get it every Saturday morning. Only I have to put down in a little book exactly how I spend it," she added.

"And that's the right way to do," Mrs. Carey announced with firmness. "The way young people scatter their money around, reckless-like, you'd think it grew on bushes. You ought to keep a record of where every penny goes and show it to your uncle every week."

"I do," said Marian meekly, and made her escape.

Dix hailed her from behind the hedge, however, before she had gone three steps.

"Aw, Marian, where you going?" he asked, his wheedling voice a certain sign that he was deserted by the older boys and would welcome an invitation to accompany her.

"I'm going uptown," Marian replied pleasantly. "Shopping."

"I'll come with you," said Dix, also pleasantly.

"I don't need you this morning, Dix," Marian explained. "I'm only going up to the dry-goods store on Main Street and there's nothing to interest you there."

Dix beamed at her persuasively.

"We could get a soda," he suggested.

Marian shrewdly suspected that he had heard fragments of her conversation with the housekeeper—voices would carry through windows, she was sure.

"I'll bring you an ice cream cone when I come back," she said diplomatically, "if you'll stay here where it is cool and shady."

"A double-decker?" bargained Dix.

"Of course, a double-decker," Marian said. "Chocolate and vanilla."

Dix succumbed to the lure of his favorite combination.

"All right," he surrendered, "only I hope you're not going to be gone all day."

"I'll be back before lunch," said Marian, avoiding a specific time limit. Dix, she knew, was capable of coming in search of her if she overstayed her leave. He was anything but punctual himself, but demanded the virtue in his friends.

Marian hurried off, intent on reaching Main Street before anything else should happen to delay her. There had been a strong reason why she had discouraged the attendance of Dix—after concluding her shopping, she meant to come home by way of the brick house where the lady in white lived.

"It's so queer no one ever speaks of her," thought Marian, turning into the crowded entrance of the drygoods shop, whose proprietor liked to display his wares outside.

The white goods section was a fascinating place and Marian lingered over her selection. She finally decided on a dotted Swiss and had it measured off and wrapped for her, before she discovered that she had forgotten to cash the money-order. The post-office was across the street, however, so that omission was easily remedied. Marian was back again in less than ten minutes, cash for her purchase tightly clutched in her hand. Then she remembered she needed lace for the neck and sleeves and a length of black velvet ribbon for a belt. These were added and she stepped out into the brilliant sunshine.

a compact parcel under her arm and her heart beating a little more quickly than usual. She was going to walk past the brick house and while nothing at all might happen, she hoped with all her might that something would.

CHAPTER XV

THE LADY IN WHITE

RALSTON AVENUE was one of the quietest streets in the quiet town of Stillwell. It was not built up as much as other sections and being one of the newer thoroughfares—"new" in the sense that the houses were more modern and the owners thereof not descendants of the original settlers—was comparatively little traveled. The trees planted by the Borough fathers were still in the stripling stage and there was none of the magnificent shade which distinguished Euclid Avenue.

Marian glanced through the iron bars of the first big gate as she neared the brick house. The garden smiled in the radiant sunshine, but not a leaf or a living thing stirred within it.

"Good morning, Still Waters," called the rich voice she remembered so vividly.

Marian stopped abruptly under the casement windows. She looked up, but could see no one.

"Are you coming to see me?" the voice asked,

a pretty hint of eagerness making it seem more hurried.

"I—I could," said Marian, feeling unaccountably shy.

A tinkling sound announced that the key had been tossed down to her.

"The gate lock turns more easily—I've had it oiled," said the lovely voice. "Do come in and see me, little Still Waters."

Marian found that the key turned more easily and the gate swung open lightly at her first attempt. She heard it click behind her as she hastened toward the white door which opened noiselessly as it had the first time.

The lady in white was just the same—the room was unchanged. As Marian's glance fell on the white knitting her hostess had evidently put aside to greet her, she saw that it was a child's sweater, but one lately started.

"So it can't be a dream," thought Marian; "that isn't the same sweater—she has finished the other one. Things don't get finished in dreams."

The lady in white drew her over to the cushioned window seat. One side of the room was taken up by the long window which looked on another garden.

"Tell me about yourself, my dear," said the

mistress of all this, taking up her knitting and beginning to knit with such speed and precision that Marian's eyes could scarcely follow the flying needles.

It was surprisingly easy to talk to her. Marian found, to her own amazement, that she had been *hungry* to talk to someone who would listen sympathetically. She told the lady in white about her beautiful young mother and about her earnest, plodding good father and of how she had kept house for him and gone to school and been very, very happy in Villyea. And she told of Aunt Edith who had too many children to "do" for another and about Uncle Cornelius and Mrs. Carey and Professor Drayton and the three lively boys who kept Euclid Avenue in a perpetually excited state. But at the mention of the boys, for the first time the attention of the lady in white seemed to wander.

"Are you like your mother?" she asked gently.

"Like my mother?" Marian stared. "Why, my mother was a Beauty!"

The lady in white smiled above her knitting, but made no comment.

"I'd be satisfied if I could just be *pretty*," said Marian sadly. "I found some poetry in the library the other day—that made me feel sorry for the girl it was written about; she must have felt as I do.

> *"'She is not fair to outward view*
> *As many maidens be.'*

"Isn't that awful, when you remember all the lovely poetry that has been written to beautiful girls?" demanded Marian earnestly.

The lady in white twitched her yarn skillfully and never slackened the pace of her busy needles.

"I'm afraid you didn't memorize the next two lines," she suggested. "Don't they run something like this:

> *"'Her loveliness I never knew,*
> *Until she smiled at me.'"*

"But that doesn't mean anything," protested Marian. "If you can't be fair to 'outward view,' nothing else matters. Mrs. Carey is always telling me about my Aunt Amelia—she says I look and act just like her. Aunt Amelia wasn't one bit pretty, but she had the largest funeral anyone ever had in Stillwell. I'd rather be lovely than have a large funeral," concluded Marian with perfect seriousness.

The lady in white threw back her head and laughed and her laughter was like chiming bells.

"We all wish to be lovely, I think," she said, sobering. "But, dear child, are you sure you knew what beauty really is? Do you think it was your mother's hair, or her eyes, or her features that made her impossible to forget?"

"Why, of course," Nancy Bolton's daughter said promptly. "See, here is her picture"—and she pulled out the locket on its slender gold chain.

"Yes, she was beautiful," agreed the lady in white, studying the charming miniature, "but she has left you her greatest gift."

Marian stared in wide-eyed astonishment.

"You don't know what I mean, do you, Still Waters?" the lady in white said softly.

Still speechless, Marian shook her head.

"Why—why do you call me that?" she managed to say presently.

"Because you remind me of still waters in quiet places," said the lady in white composedly. "The first time I saw you, I felt it—I could have let the sweater lie on the grass until one of the gardeners came along to pick it up for me. But when I saw you, I knew you were sunny and quiet. I am fond of sunshine—and of peace."

Marian did not understand very clearly, but she was not at all afraid. She folded her hands in her lap and waited.

"I have lived alone for twelve years," said the lady in white. "No one had been inside my door, during that time, until you came."

"But you said my mother left me her gift," Marian groped, her mind clinging to that, for her, unbelievable statement.

"Charm," said the lady in white. "Oh, perhaps not her own peculiar charm; as you describe her to me, your mother must have been a creature of fire and dash and spirit. That is why she is remembered—for the spirit that made her beauty vivid. But there are as many ways to be lovely as there are girls in the world— you have a sunny spirit, a lovely serenity and graciousness that is just as wonderful and just as much a gift as your mother's flaming personality. You can be beautiful too—but it will be as Marian Blessing, not as Nancy Bolton."

Marian's straight brows drew together reflectively.

"Do not try to puzzle it out in one short morning," her new friend counseled her tolerantly. "Just turn the thoughts over and over in your mind and some day the whole meaning will be clear to you. And now don't you want to see my gardens?"

Marian rose with the inimitable grace that was one of her unconscious charms—nothing ever fluttered or flapped when she moved about.

"I'd love to see your flowers," she said sincerely, "but I promised to be home in time for lunch—and I have to go back and get an ice cream cone for Dix. Will you show me the gardens another morning?"

The lady in white shrank back a little.

"Oh, I never go out," she said. "But you shall have a key—there are often times when I do not feel like talking, but that is no reason why you should not enjoy the flowers. Take the gate key and feel free to come in as often as you like—if I do not call to you you will know that I am—busy. Come as often as you like and pick as many bouquets as you wish—there is an abundance of flowers and sometimes they are wasted—if flowers can be wasted. I will speak to the gardeners, so you will be asked no questions. You will like the gardens, Still Waters."

She smiled at Marian and held out the gate key on a very small white palm. Marian took it, feeling more than ever as though she were dreaming or reading a fairy tale, and holding it tightly in one hand and her package in the other, said "Good-by." It was characteristic of Marian that she did not talk a great deal and when confused or bewildered, less than ever.

The white door closed behind her.

"It's my secret," she sang lightly to herself, as she went back to Main Street to get the promised cone for the waiting Dix.

"It's my secret and I won't tell anyone—I have a key and a garden that no one knows about —and I can go there whenever I please. She—" Marian broke off in dismay as she remembered that she did not know the name of the lady in white.

"I'll find out, the next time I see her," she thought. "I suppose if I asked, the Drayton boys could tell me—but they wouldn't stop until they had asked fifty questions. No, I'll wait and find it out for myself."

Dix was delighted with his cone and forebore to reproach the giver for her prolonged absence. Indeed Marian found that she was fifteen minutes late for lunch, but Mrs. Carey declared that she knew what shopping did to one's sense of time.

"When I get in a store, seems like I never know enough to come home," she observed.

"That's dotted Swiss, you bought, isn't it? Yes, I call it right pretty, but I don't see how you're going to make it. I'm considerably older than you and I never made myself a dress yet."

This was quite true. Mrs. Carey belonged to that rapidly decreasing number of women to whom the secrets of dressmaking and millinery forever remain unfathomable mysteries. The housekeeper had never bought a ready-made dress in her life. She could sew exquisitely, but to fit a dress was something, she thought, that called for special skill and training. She "had the dressmaker" twice a year, as regularly as she cleaned house, and the carefully stitched frocks this seamstress turned out for her were worn year after year, with absolute indifference to the whims of changing fashions, until they were consigned to the rag-bag. It was the same with her hats—Mrs. Carey never touched a hat to alter it in any way, once the Stillwell milliner had fitted her out with new headgear. If she decided, on returning home, that a feather would be more becoming, say two inches to the right of a buckle, Mrs. Carey would never think of moving the feather; she might destroy the mysterious charm of a trimmed hat. She always went back to the milliner and watched her, half fearfully, as the feather was uprooted and moved.

So she watched Marian with ill-concealed admiration as she spread out her material on the dining-room table after lunch and pinned her pattern in place. Marian would have preferred to work alone, for she was none too confident of her own ability and she had to read the directions several times to make sure she understood them, but she knew that Mrs. Carey's interest was kindly meant.

"Mrs. Armstrong would let you sew it on her machine," said Mrs. Carey when the cutting was finished.

There was no machine in the Bolton household, but Marian did not mind. Haste was not her object and though she could manipulate a sewing machine, she was more familiar with hand sewing. She would make the dress by hand, but she did not intend to sew on it that afternoon.

"I must do some more on those notes," she said firmly. "The Professor will need them and yet he wouldn't say a word if I spent weeks and weeks over them. Sewing can wait—though I do feel just like sewing this afternoon," she added wistfully, patting the neatly folded pieces with fingers that fairly itched to get at the necessary basting.

CHAPTER XVI

FAIRY GARDENS

"I DON'T see as you'll ever get that dress done," Mrs. Carey remarked several times in the days that followed.

She herself liked to "keep at a thing," as she expressed it, until it was finished and out of the way. It irritated her vaguely to see how Marian apparently flitted from one task to another and, worse still, allowed herself to be interrupted when once settled down to sewing.

The first half of the notes were in order now and Marian had taken them to the gratified Professor, who was so pleased his thanks became slightly incoherent. Marian had discovered a great box of clippings at his elbow and, after much persuasion, had borne them away to be sorted and classified at her leisure. Donald, it developed, had once tried to make a file for his father, but orderliness was not one of his talents and he had merely succeeded in upsetting the mucilage, tearing precious items and losing others.

In addition to this clerical work, the mending continued steadily. Not even for the joy of working on her new dress, could Marian be persuaded to give up the patching and darning that made such a difference in the collective appearance of the Drayton family wardrobes. Since the work must continue a secret, she did it mostly in her own room and in the afternoon. And since she was mindful of the Mayor's command that she spend several hours in the open air, the mornings were given up to carrying out this order.

While Donald and Dix did not wish to be surfeited with feminine society—David never considered the question but continued to amuse himself alone, how no one knew—at times they were ready and willing to admit a girl to their games, especially a girl who, like Marian, would not cry if she fell out of the hay loft and who had a positive talent for making iced lemonade at almost any hour in the day.

But, strangely enough, when they sought Marian lately, she was not to be found. Mrs. Carey invariably said she had gone "uptown" and Mart Powers responded with the vague information that he had seen her lately, but she was "off." It was exasperating when the two boys were actually willing to include Marian in their plans, not to have her on hand to include.

It was the gardens belonging to Mrs. Neal—for Marian had asked the lady in white and learned her name—that drew Marian. It was the most delightful thing that had ever happened in her rather colorless life—this having a key dropped into her lap and with it the right to visit such gardens as she had never dreamed of. Sometimes, in her visits, she saw Mrs. Neal —always a beautiful figure, always dressed in white and with the inevitable white knitting in her hands or somewhere, ready to be picked up— but oftener the lovely voice was silent and unless she was called from the windows, Marian never went to the white door.

She never forgot her first visit to the place after the key had been given to her. It was two or three mornings after her talk with the lady in white and Marian felt as though she must be a fairy princess as she fitted the key in the lock, saw it turn and slipped inside the iron gate. She had never walked past the white door and now, as she did so, she glanced at the house. White curtains were blowing gently in the breeze, but there was no sign of life about the house.

Marian walked until she reached the end of the house and gave a little gasp.

The grounds stretched before her, as far as her eyes could see. There were no fences, only interlocking gardens and terraces. She was standing on a terrace bordered with boxwood and wide, stone steps led down to a sunken garden, brilliant with flowers arranged in formal beds which had, for the center of the design, a shallow pool.

"How lovely!" said Marian aloud. "How lovely!"

She went down the steps slowly and sat on the white marble bench beside the pool. Birds were drinking and they merely tilted their small heads as if to satisfy themselves that she was comfortable, then calmly returned to their sipping. It was clear that they did not fear being disturbed.

"I wonder if people in Stillwell know about this," thought Marian, and then her eyes espied another flight of steps and she felt a great curiosity to know where they led.

She went up and found herself in a rose garden, a bewildering riot of color and fragrance, with great bees humming above the roses as though they rejoiced at finding such honey ready for the gathering. Marian had never seen such roses, perfect specimens, watered and tended till they blossomed without flaw—and then withered and fell to the ground. Some bushes, of the early blooming varieties, were surrounded by little heaps of satin petals, mute testimony to the sad little story of the rose that has no one to admire it.

This was as far as Marian went on her first visit and all that afternoon, while she copied deadly dull paragraphs for the Professor—how could he be interested in Greek and Latin, she wondered, when she was reading a living fairy story that she was sure would grow more interesting the further she went!—she tried to guess what might lie beyond the rose garden.

A day or two later she found out. It was thrilling to let herself in with the key, to wait a few minutes to hear if the wonderful voice called to her, then in silence to skirt the sunken garden, bury her face in a mass of pink tea roses as she passed the rose garden—and from there she stepped into a place her own great-grandmother might have planted. Only Marian knew nothing about her great-grandmother's garden.

Pinks and marigolds, phlox, Sweet William, Canterbury bells—all the old, old posies, growing its riotous profusion. There were brick walks and narrow grass borders between the beds and there was no formal arrangement. At one end was a wine-red brick wall and gorgeous hollyhocks flowered against this background. In the center of the wall was an arch and set in this arch, a little white gate.

Marian peeped over the gate.

She saw a vegetable garden that would make Peter Parsons or Mart Powers quite green with envy. Beyond the vegetable garden was a glimpse of orchards and more velvet lawns.

"Oh!" said Marian, perceiving that there was a man working among the vegetables.

He turned and lifted his battered straw hat when he saw her.

"Mrs. Neal said I could visit her gardens," said Marian, smiling her friendly smile. "Aren't they beautiful!"

"Very fine," the man answered, leaning on his hoe. "Very fine. You're the little Miss Blessing Mrs. Neal wrote of in her note."

"Did she write about me?" said Marian, puzzled. "How—funny."

The man glanced at her oddly. He was deeply tanned by the sun and his face was wrinkled, but he moved about much more quickly than white. Why didn't she go out and see her flowers?

"Why don't you pick some posies for yourself?" Mrs. Neal suggested, substituting for the unspoken question one of her own. "Take armfuls, if you like—the gardeners tell me there is more than we can ever use, though I send boxes every day to the hospitals."

"Your gardener asked me to pick bouquets," said Marian slowly, "but, Mrs. Neal, if I take home flowers, Uncle Cornelius will ask me where I got them; not that I do not want him to know —only this way it is a secret. The nicest secret I ever had. And—and—I thought you wouldn't mind if it stayed a secret—at least for a little while."

"I like secrets, too," Mrs. Neal affirmed, putting a cool hand for a moment over Marian's little tanned one.

"We'll keep this as our secret—you and I. I should not like to be talked about—perhaps this is the better way."

So Marian continued to go and come, using her key each time with a delicious sense of letting herself into a fortress or castle, and the Drayton boys puzzled as to what could take her "uptown" so often and detain her for so many hours.

"Play dominoes with me, Marian," Dix would beg.

"Now, Dix, you know I want to copy those notes for your father," Marian would remind him.

"Do it at night—" Dix rattled the dominoes persuasively.

"Uncle Cornelius won't let me—he says it is daytime work," said Marian, and her tone gave no indication of the resentment she had felt when Mayor Bolton first laid down this rule.

"Then do 'em in the morning," Dix would suggest, being a resourceful young person and fairly sure of obtaining his own way in the end.

"Oh, all right—I did intend to sew on my dress," capitulated Marian.

It was a close, muggy afternoon and Dix was not particularly patient. She played seven games with him, made lemonade when Donald, hot and tired from a grilling ball game, slouched up the steps and took a tall glass over to the Professor, certain she would find him, with the windows closed, hard at work on his book.

"That was very refreshing," he said appreciatively, as he handed back the glass. "You're a refreshing personality, Marian."

As she crossed the lawn she met David, soaking wet to his knees and with his face plastered with mud and what looked like mosquito bites.

"Lemonade, Dave?" she called pleasantly.

"No—thanks," he said, without turning his head.

Dix drank David's share of the lemonade with ill-concealed satisfaction.

Marian, absorbed in her own thoughts, did not see him sit down with the pitcher between his knees and "fish" for the pieces of ice at the bottom. Donald watched his younger brother for a few moments in silence.

"Why don't you eat the pitcher?" he suggested at length, sarcastically.

Dix made a face at him, Marian automatically rescued the pitcher and hostilities were averted by a division of the few crackers remaining on the pretty china plate.

"Doesn't David like sweet things?" asked Marian, beginning to gather up the glasses.

"He doesn't like folks," Dix volunteered, which was perhaps the answer to a question Marian had not asked.

CHAPTER XVII

MARIAN MAKES A RESCUE

STILLWELL was fond of boasting that the nights were "always cool," but the heat of the afternoon seemed to be intensified after sunset. Mayor Bolton came home, tired and more preoccupied than usual, changed into white linen and sat moodily in the library, going over a sheaf of papers, until the dinner gong sounded.

A bowl of nasturtiums made a flaming ring in the center of the table and the appetizing dinner was exquisitely served by Mrs. Carey, who knew to a nicety the trick of having the hot foods very hot and the cold things iced; but the Mayor had little appetite and once or twice he passed his hand across his forehead in a weary gesture that roused the sympathy of his observant niece.

"Have—have you a headache, Uncle Cornelius?" she asked.

Marian always found it a trifle difficult to ask

her uncle a direct question. As a rule she waited until he had started a conversation.

"A headache?" he repeated. "Why—no; but it has been a hard day in town and I'd like to get out of going to that meeting to-night; no sense to having these affairs up for decision in midsummer."

Marian knew he meant the Council meetings, but what the "affairs" they were to decide, she had no way of guessing. She knew that the Council met in the second story of a gray, stone building—the Borough Hall—on Main Street, and she sensed instinctively how warm the room would be, with all the electric lights turned on and perhaps a debate being launched between some of the councilmen.

"I suppose you have to go?" she hinted a bit timidly.

"Can't escape," said the Mayor sadly. "I wouldn't complain, nor would Singleton, if there were the slightest chance of getting what we are fighting for; but women—you can't do a thing with them," he finished, smiling across the table at one in the making who only grinned at this slur on her sex.

He was off, presently, for the Hall and Marian dutifully helped Mrs. Carey with the dishes, a regular service which was sincerely appreciated, for the housekeeper was tired at the end of her busy day. She could have had someone come in to help her and indeed her employer had suggested it more than once, but unfortunately Mrs. Carey was one of those industrious mortals who prefer to do everything themselves and do not like, or perhaps cannot, explain their methods to another.

After the work was done, Marian went out on the porch to sit quietly till the nine o'clock whistle blew. Mrs. Carey declared that she needed a walk and went to see her confidante, Miss Palmer. It was barely dark by nine, for daylight saving was practiced in Stillwell, but Marian went up to her room as the mill whistle sounded—after all, getting ready for bed could be prolonged and sitting by herself on the porch was not exactly a thrilling way to spend the summer evening. She could hear Dix wrangling with Peter over the question of going to bed and knew when he was forcibly captured and carried off, by his staccato shrieks. Dix usually performed in this manner every evening and Marian was sure that more than half the time he got out of bed and came downstairs to play on the porch in his pajamas, after Peter had gone for his nightly game of checkers with Mart Powers, who lived in a little two-roomed house on one of the near-by side streets.

"That's Donald's whistle," said Marian to herself, kneeling by the window and peering out into the dusk, now lighted by myriads of fireflies.

"He's going to the movies with that King boy—but Dave isn't with them. My goodness, what would Uncle Cornelius say if I did half the things the Draytons do? But then he always knows where I am and the Professor doesn't seem to bother."

The lanky forms of Donald and his chum disappeared and Marian began to read and undress, an accomplishment which required more time than skill. But the light made the room warm and she soon snapped it off and completed her preparations in the soft gloom. She lay quietly in bed for a little while, thinking of the lady in white and her gardens; of the smiling picture in the living room downstairs; of her uncle Cornelius at the Council meeting; of the rebellious little Dix. In the midst of wondering whether to put an extra row of tucking on the sleeves of her dotted Swiss—still in the stages of being made—Marian fell asleep.

When she woke, she did not know what time it was, but the air was cooler. She thought perhaps it was near morning. The inevitable desire that impels us all to know what the clock says, the moment we wake from sleep, urged her to patter across the room and consult the tiny celluloid clock on the dresser.

Quarter of twelve!

Then she heard a noise that she now realized had been sounding intermittently. Probably it had wakened her, though she had not consciously heard it.

"Meow! Me-ow!"—the wail was thin but piercing.

"A kitten!" Marian peered through the screen in a futile endeavor to see the unhappy little animal.

The wailing continued and presently Marian concluded that the kitten must be caught in a tree. She knew how a young cat, when frightened, will climb to the top of a tree in its frantic efforts to escape, or even to get to the ground. This mewing sounded as though the kitten might be in one of the trees near the house, or caught in some place from which it could not extricate itself.

"I wonder if Uncle Cornelius is home yet?" speculated Marian.

She opened the door into the hall and looked out. The light downstairs was still burning, a sign that the Mayor had not yet come in. From Mrs. Carey's room, across the hall, came an unmistakable noise, not loud, or startling, but regular and—it must be admitted, rasping. Mrs. Carey was rather proud of the fact that she never snored after midnight—she solemnly affirmed that she might snore "a little" before the magic hour of twelve, but after that, she would tell you, she slept as quietly as a kitten.

The simile made Marian smile to herself in the darkness. It was the kitten who was making the greater noise now.

She began to dress quietly. She would go down and find out where the unhappy animal was imprisoned. To be sure, she was not very experienced when it came to climbing trees, but she thought she could manage to climb if it had to be done. She had a pet theory that whatever had to be done, one somehow accomplished.

When she was ready, she went quietly out and down the stairs, noticing how loudly the clock in the living room ticked, though in the sounds of the normal day it went quite unnoticed. As soon as she stepped out on the side porch, Marian knew that the mewing kitten was somewhere at the back of the house.

She had not known how beautiful and still a summer's night was at this hour. Not a leaf of the shrubbery stirred and, as soon as her eyes were accustomed to the darkness, she found that it was not black, but almost a luminous half-light in which she could see to walk the gravel path with ease. The air was a little damp and sweet with the mingled scent of many flowers. Miles away she heard a dog barking and several blocks over a car, filled with a laughing group of gay riders dashed through—their voices came to her softened by the distance. Glancing up at the Drayton house, she saw a dim light burning in the room where the Professor usually worked. He was probably straining his eyes under the flickering gas jet and it was safe to assume that a dozen kittens might have been wailing on his front porch and he would not have heard them.

"Kitty!" called Marian under her breath. "Here, Kitty, Kitty, what's the matter?"

The mewing stopped for a brief second, then began again.

"Why, you're up the maple tree," said Marian, guided by the noise to the sturdy young maple tree that was planted in the center of the drive where it turned at the garage doors.

"I should think you could get yourself down from there," went on Marian, addressing the unseen kitten with more severity. "That isn't such a tall tree—can't you come down if you use a little sense and try? Come on, Kitty, Kitty!"

But Kitty perversely went a few more inches nearer to the top. Marian could hear the leaves rustling and the outline of the tree moved slightly. The mewing sounded more plaintively.

"I see I have to climb that tree," Marian murmured. "Well, thank goodness, it is dark and none of the boys can see me—Donald would laugh himself into fits if he ever saw me trying to 'shinny up.'"

She caught hold of one of the lower branches and pulled herself up into the tree. She would have preferred a little more light, even though the darkness was friendly to her awkward efforts, but as it was she managed to work her way cautiously toward the top of the tree. She continued to speak soothingly to the kitten and she tried not to think of the ants—or worse yet, the caterpillars—she might be mashing as she felt her way. Marian did not care for ants or bugs of any kind and the Drayton boys often laughed at what Donald dubbed her "squeamishness."

It was rather ticklish work, feeling her way through the thick foliage and testing each branch before she trusted her weight to it. Three or four times the mewing sounded so close that she put out her hand, expecting to touch a soft, furry body. Each time she closed it on empty air.

At last a pathetic "Meow!" almost in her ear made her jump and impulsively she grabbed at a branch above her head. She was rewarded by a long-drawn out howl of anguish and what felt like a handful of steel wires encased in fur. The kitten was clinging desperately to the only refuge it knew.

There are more comfortable situations imaginable than to be at the top of a slender tree which gives with every movement of one's body, in the dead of night, with a weak-minded kitten —so Marian wrathfully was inclined to catalogue the unfortunate creature—and easier tasks than to get oneself and the said kitten safely down the tree.

Marian's greatest difficulty was in detaching the kitten from the branch to which it clung with every tiny sharpened claw on four determined small feet. Once lifted clear of the branch, those claws betrayed every intention of digging into the first surface offered and Marian had no wish to be the sacrifice. She rested precariously in a narrow crotch and tried to soothe the kitten with words and smooth it into some sort of tranquillity.

It was a very young kitten, she judged, and she could feel its heart pounding against its small ribs, as though the beats would burst through the slender body. The girl realized the abject terror of the little creature and patiently and quietly stroked it and whispered encouragement, until it consented to nestle peacefully against her.

She held the kitten with one hand and used the other to steady herself as she began the descent. She had to stop twice to release the kitten's claws which scratched her sharply as he dug in with the instinct of self-preservation. She moved very slowly and she was almost down when she thought she saw something moving on the lawn.

"It must be a dog," she thought, clutching the kitten a little more tightly. "I hope the cat doesn't see it—he might get excited and begin to scratch me."

She thought she felt the kitten slipping and,

not being minded to drop her burden—though any member of the cat family can be trusted to land right-side up under the most trying circumstances—she retreated a notch or two, to make adjustments.

"It may not be a dog—but it moves like one," breathed Marian in the kitten's ear. "Wouldn't it be nice if he should camp at the foot of this tree and wait for us. I've heard of dogs doing that for hours at a time."

The kitten remained quiet and Marian decided to proceed.

Cautiously she put out one foot, slipped down, and stood poised on the last bough. Then she jumped.

As she landed on the springy turf, she turned quickly to see if any dog was prowling about. Something ran against her with terrific force and knocked her flat.

"Me-ow-ow!" snarled the kitten who was certainly not having a pleasant evening.

Marian said nothing, but lay perfectly still.

CHAPTER XVIII

GLORY RIVER

"GOOD grief!" it was David's voice. "You might know it would be you!"

He hauled Marian to her feet and not even the darkness could hide the manifest disapproval with which he gazed upon her. He did not ask if he had hurt her—his attitude was that some explanation was due him. Girls, his expression and voice indicated, had no business to be out at that time of night, obstructing the right of way of energetic neighbors.

"I was getting a kitten out of the maple tree," said Marian meekly, sensing his expectation of an apology.

"Well, do you know what time it is?" he demanded savagely. "It's after twelve—that's how late it is. After twelve—and here you are parading around on the back lawn."

"I wasn't parading," Marian declared firmly. "I heard a poor little kitten mewing and I came out to see where it was: and you pretty nearly smashed it, knocking me down on top of it like that."

"Cats have nine lives—you can't hurt 'em," said David callously.

He looked at her oddly. In the indistinct light she could see that his face was dripping with perspiration and he was breathing heavily as though he had been running.

"I suppose you'll have it blabbed all around town by morning that you saw me coming home to-night," he suggested curtly.

Marian had never understood him, but that did not prevent her from understanding what he was trying to ask.

"I won't tell a soul if you don't want me to," she said gently.

"Say, Marian, do you mean that?" David begged, his voice hoarse with his effort to speak in an undertone.

"Honestly, won't you tell—not a single soul? If you tell on me, you'll just spoil everything, that's what you'll do."

"I won't tell—I promise you I won't tell," said Marian gravely.

"Good for you—don't forget," David shot back and then, without a word as to whether she was all right, or a glance at her or the rescued kitten, he vaulted over the hedge and into his own yard.

Marian stood where he had left her. She saw a dark figure, hardly more than a blot outlined against the corner of the house, follow the rain pipe up to a second-story window and disappear after fumbling a few moments, doubtless with a window screen.

So that was the way David got in when he was out late at night!

"Well—I might as well give the kitten some milk and put it to bed," said Marian to herself, turning toward the back porch.

She found milk in the refrigerator, decided that it would be a waste of time to warm it on such a night and fed the kitten a saucerful. He seemed very glad to get it and was quite willing to cuddle down in an empty starch box Marian found and hastily outfitted with a piece of flannel, more for its softness than for warmth.

"Now you stay nicely on the back porch till morning," she admonished her charge, depositing him and the box under the bench where Mrs. Carey liked to sit to "get a breath of air."

"In the morning you may be adopted—if you're good."

Marian latched the screen door, closed and

locked the kitchen door and went on into the front hall, anxious to regain her own room and make up for lost sleep.

"Marian!" said an astonished voice.

It was Mayor Bolton and Marian had been too intent on arranging for the comfort of the kitten to hear the wheels of his car or to see his lights as he drove into the garage while she was busy in the kitchen. No wonder the Mayor was slightly startled to meet his niece, fully dressed, at half past twelve when he supposed her to have been asleep for several hours.

"I came down," explained Marian, fortunately unconscious of a smudge on her right cheek and a three-cornered tear in the skirt of her dress, "to get a kitten that was crying. I had to climb a tree to reach him, but he's asleep on the back porch now."

"I see," the Mayor assured her, but his thoughts were so evidently on something else, that it was hardly possible to mistake his interest for other than perfunctory listening.

Marian had never seen him look more tired. His immaculate collar was wilted and as he leaned against the newel post she heard him sigh, a sigh of utter mental and physical weariness.

"Uncle Cornelius, there's ginger ale in the ice

box," she said impulsively. "Let me get it for you—I'll bring it out to you on the porch."

"I suppose I'll drink it if it's brought to me," assented the Mayor, "but I wouldn't take three extra steps to-night to find a fortune."

Instead of going out on the porch, he wandered into the living room and sank into one of the chairs there and he was still sitting in the dark when Marian returned with a tray. On the spur of the moment she had made two sandwiches from cold sliced chicken she had found in the ice chest and the tall glass of ginger ale tinkled refreshingly.

"Here, here, this is altogether wrong," protested the Mayor, rousing himself as she turned on a deeply shaded floor lamp that gave a pleasant glow and no glare whatever.

"I should have come out and cracked the ice for you—where's your glass, child?"

"I don't care for any—and it's easy to chip ice—Mrs. Carey has a chopper thing," said Marian, putting down her tray on one end of the long table.

"Sandwiches!" the Mayor was plainly pleased. "I don't believe I'm hungry, but these look good. We had a warm session to-night."

Marian curled up on the divan and waited.

The Mayor ate half a sandwich before he seemed to be aware of her presence again.

"You ought to go to bed," he said, staring reflectively at his glass. "Much too late for youngsters your age to be up and about. Singleton asked me about you to-night—Marian, do you know anything about the river?"

Marian was surprised at this abrupt change of topics, but she managed to reply that she had heard of the Glory River, but had never seen it.

"No, I don't suppose you have," said her uncle. "I've always meant to take you down the river road some afternoon, but I haven't had time so far; these special meetings play the mischief with my schedule."

"What an odd name—'Glory River,'" Marian commented.

"It was named for old Tom Glory who fished it from the tributary creek at its head, to the sea," said the Mayor. "Well, Glory River has caused Stillwell more sorrow and trouble than any pleasure it ever gave Tom Glory is worth."

He began on the second sandwich.

"Know anything about playgrounds?" he shot at his waiting niece.

"Oh, yes," said Marian, glad she could answer promptly. "In Villyea, there was a beautiful playground, with three teachers. In vacation time it was open all the day; the little children had it in the morning and the grammar school boys and girls had it afternoon. The high school students could dance from seven to nine in the evening. They had sandpiles and a baseball diamond and tents where they held sewing and basket-making classes. It was lovely."

"Stillwell hasn't a single playground, large or small," her uncle declared. "There is a conservative element that argues the town doesn't need a playground; their theory is that the children should seek the woods and fields if they haven't large gardens of their own, and that Nature will take care of them and automatically guarantee them health and safety."

"Do they?" asked Marian excitedly.

The Mayor put down his tall glass, now empty.

"No—no more, thank you," he said as she started to rise. "Do they what?"

"Seek the woods and fields."

Mayor Bolton laughed, a little grimly.

"They seek the Glory River," was his answer. "It's safe to say there isn't a mother in town who at some time has not spent an afternoon or perhaps a day, worrying lest her youngsters have fallen into the river and been drowned. The

Glory is a mile from town, but it's like a magnet—it draws the boys who can swim and those who think they can; younger brothers and sisters troop after them. Not a summer goes by without its quota of narrow escapes and last year two little fellows lost their lives.

"I've nothing to say against the use of the river for sports for those old enough to look out for themselves," went on the Mayor and the councilmen would have recognized his "fighting voice,"—"let the young people canoe and swim and hold their carnivals there. All well and good—but a river is no playground for little folk and something must be done about it. Now—this summer!"

Marian thought of the vast number of special meetings which had absorbed her busy uncle's leisure evening time.

"Don't they do anything about it at the meetings?" she suggested.

"Not much but talk," said the Mayor bitterly. "Or I shouldn't say that—we've overcome objections to the playground to the extent that we have obtained the necessary backing. We see our way clear to financing the project. We even have the site selected and Mr. Singleton and two or three other wealthy men have agreed to equip the place completely. Talk does accomplish wonders, if properly persisted in."

He drifted off into a reverie of his own and Marian, who was momentarily dreading being sent to bed before she heard the entire story, ventured to call him back.

"Why don't you get the playground then?" she asked eagerly.

"We're blocked," her uncle declared somberly. "There's just one logical location in town for the kind of playground we have in mind; we want more land than is allowed for the ordinary playfield. The plan is to devote part of the plot to athletics, part to a wading pool which can easily be constructed, and divide the remaining parts into sections which a variety of interests will call for. There is just one tract of land in Stillwell available for the playground and we cannot get hold of it."

"Oh, why, Uncle Cornelius"—Marian's tone was sharp with anxiety.

He looked at her and a curious little smile showed in his eyes.

"Getting you all worked up, I see," he said humorously. "Well, Marian, the only difficulty in the way is, unfortunately, the hardest to surmount. The owner of this desirable piece of property doesn't wish to sell it. In fact, she flatly refuses to sell it or listen to any conversation on the subject."

"Make her listen," urged Marian. "Can't someone write her a letter?"

"Mr. Singleton has had a voluminous correspondence with the lady on the subject," the Mayor explained, "and I myself have attempted to make our plans clear. She is not interested and I must say she doesn't leave us in doubt as to her disinclination to talk of the project."

"You could go and see her—couldn't you?" submitted Marian, forgetting to be timid in her eagerness to have the right kind of a playground in Stillwell.

"Dix might go to Glory River and be drowned," she was thinking swiftly. "Maybe that is where David goes so much—I wonder if he can swim?"

"I have been to see this property holder," the tired voice of the Mayor was recounting.

"And she said she wouldn't sell her ground?" Marian asked, hastily abandoning her own thoughts.

"She didn't have to say it. She refused to see me."

"Oh!" Marian was really shocked.

Refuse to see the Mayor of her own town. Why the lady who owned the desirable property couldn't be very polite.

"I doubt if anyone in Stillwell has seen her, to speak to, since she came here to live," said Mayor Bolton, musingly.

"She is rumored to have had a great trouble and to have come here to live in seclusion. Marian, you must go to bed—what am I thinking of, to keep you up like this? You're almost asleep this minute."

Marian moved obediently toward the stairs and her uncle snapped off the light.

"I'll make one more effort in the morning," he said, as she started up. "I think I'll go once more and try to get an interview with Mrs. Neal."

CHAPTER XIX

SECRETS

MARIAN'S feet mechanically carried her up to her room, but her mind was occupied with a host of unanswered questions.

"Mrs. Neal!" she thought frantically, as she prepared the second time for bed.

"Mrs. Neal!" she muttered sleepily as she crept between the cool sheets and closed her eyes. "Does Mrs. Neal own the land Uncle Cornelius wants for a playground? And why won't she sell it, I wonder?"

But in the morning, the question of the playground receded temporarily, to be replaced by speculations regarding David Drayton. At breakfast, Mayor Bolton and his niece were interrupted by an extremely irate gentleman who assured Mrs. Carey that he couldn't wait and didn't intend to wait, for anyone to finish eating. No, he had no appointment with the Mayor and as a taxpayer he didn't need one.

"That settles it," said the Mayor, who had been listening to the altercation in his front hall.

"Once the gentle taxpayer begins to recall his assessments, the politician might as well give in gracefully. Come in, Robbins," he called, raising his voice.

Mr. Robbins was so full of his grievance that he burst into speech before he came in sight of His Honor. Marian was contented to be ignored and went quietly on with her breakfast.

"One of my cottages, over by the river has been broken into," she heard as the taxpayer came down the hall and then, as he gained the doorway—"I want to know what is going to be done about it!"

"Won't you sit down?" suggested Mayor Bolton. "How much damage has been done? When was the cottage entered? Whom do you suspect?"

Mr. Robbins answered the last question first.

"Boys!" he said explosively. "The young varmints! I was around doing some work there till eight or nine o'clock last night and everything was all right. Six o'clock this morning I found the padlock broken and the furnishings of the house turned upside down. I know some of the smart Alecs did it, for they cooked eggs in the kitchen: boys have to stop and eat, no matter what they're up to."

"Then the mischief was done, we'll say between nine o'clock last night and six this morning," mused the Mayor. "Why, Marian—anything wrong, dear?"

"I—I dropped my napkin," Marian stammered.

All the blood in her body, she thought, poured into her face as she retrieved the square of linen. She had remembered David and his anxiety that no one should know she had seen him.

"I'll start an investigation, Robbins," promised the Mayor, "but vandalism of this kind is always hard to trace; as you say, it was probably the work of boys and the best insurance is either to put a watchman out there, as long as you have vacant cottages, or else see to it that the locks are proof against tampering."

"I pay taxes," Mr. Robbins announced grimly, "and I'm entitled to proper police protection. If I have to get a guard, he'll have orders to shoot the first trespasser he sees."

With this ultimatum he departed and breakfast was finished in peace.

Marian had intended to go and see Mrs. Neal that morning, but sober reflection convinced her that if her uncle carried out his intention of seeking an interview, the lady in white might not be disposed to listen to two ambassadors who presented their briefs so closely on each other's heels. She had still a great mass of clippings to paste and classify for the Professor and she worked patiently at these, determined to wait the outcome of her uncle's interview with Mrs. Neal, before she said anything herself.

"Not that I can hope to do any good," thought Marian, as she trimmed the ragged edges of the clippings, "but at least she may tell me why she doesn't wish to sell her land to the town."

But as soon as she saw her uncle that evening, Marian knew he had had no success. He was very silent at dinner and immediately afterward announced that he was driving out to see Mr. Singleton and would not return till late. He did not offer to take Marian with him.

The next few days were stormy and Marian, who had planned to sew on her dress, found herself called upon to entertain Dix, and at times, Donald. Neither boy was at all backward in seeking her company when time hung heavy on his hands. David did not join them in the barn or in the games they played on the porches and Marian wondered what he could possibly find to do that engaged his attention so completely. Peter Parsons was grateful, and so was the Professor, to the young neighbor who was so willing to interest and amuse the two boys who would otherwise have "turned the house topsy-turvy," a performance, Peter assured Marian, which had hitherto been expected as an accompaniment of each rainy period.

It was nearly a week later that Marian awoke from a sound sleep to hear the door of her bedroom banging at uneven intervals. She had not latched it securely and the draft from the hall was making it rattle against the lock.

"Perhaps there is a storm coming up," thought Marian, remembering that there had not been a breath of wind stirring when she went to bed.

She pattered over to the bureau and consulted the clock. Half past one. If Mrs. Carey had left the window up at the end of the hall, the screen might blow out and startle the household as it crashed. That had happened once or twice this summer.

Marian opened her door and slipped out into the hall. The weather had changed suddenly and a strong, cold wind was sweeping through the passageway. The window at the end of the hall was up and Marian knew she could close it noiselessly, for in the well-built house the window frames went up or down at one's lightest touch.

Marian took out the screen and leaned out to watch the tree tops swaying in the wind. Someone was creeping cautiously through the back yard—she thought she knew who it was. Sure enough, the slight dark form leaped the hedge and appeared a moment later, climbing the rain pipe.

"David!" whispered Marian, and the sound of her own whisper frightened her.

She closed the window hastily and went back to bed.

"Robbins has had more trouble with his cottages," said Mayor Bolton at the breakfast table. "He had me at the telephone at half past six this morning, to tell me another one has been broken into and every room thoroughly and deliberately ransacked. I believe he has four cottages not rented this year and it would seem that the boys —if boys they are—have seized upon them as a new field for their explorations."

Marian listened silently. Would David do such a thing? He might, she admitted, "for the fun of it," but it was hardly likely that one boy would wreck a cottage on any pretext. And David apparently had little to do with other boys

—he was never seen with what Dix delighted to refer to as "our gang," in blissful ignorance that he was not admitted to the ranks.

The morning was a beautiful one—clear and cool and flooded with sunshine. Marian knew how the gardens behind the iron fence would look on a morning like this and she made up her mind to go and see the flowers, even if the lady in white should remain invisible. But fortune favored her and as she closed the iron gate gently behind her, the lovely voice called softly.

"Still Waters! Have you time to come in and see me a few minutes this perfect morning?"

"It is a perfect morning, isn't it?" said Marian, as she sat down on her favorite window seat and the lady in white picked up the white knitting her busy hands seldom abandoned.

"Still Waters," said her hostess suddenly, "do you ever wonder about me?"

Marian's honest eyes answered for her.

"I suppose you do," said the lady in white a little sadly. "And I have had several letters from your uncle recently. It is very strange that when all one asks is to be allowed to live in peace that the world will persist in urging its selfish interests."

Marian swallowed desperately. She had

planned an earnest, calm speech in which she meant to set forth the ideals of the playground and explain what it was the Council wanted to do and why. But now she found herself so desperately eager to make Mrs. Neal understand that the words bubbled out in an involuntary rush.

"Oh, Mrs. Neal, Stillwell needs a playground so the children won't go to the river and be drowned!" she cried, and was alarmed at the look that came into the lovely face of the lady in white.

"A river!" whispered Mrs. Neal. "Is there a river?"

Marian nodded, wondering what she had done.

"The Glory River," she explained. "I've never seen it, but Uncle Cornelius says all the children are crazy to get to it and their mothers worry all the time. And last year two boys were drowned. The Common Council thinks if there was a large playground in town, the children would play there. Then everyone would know where they were and the mothers wouldn't have to worry."

The lady in white made no reply, but sat silently thinking. Marian waited and presently Mrs. Neal rose.

"I'll be back directly," she said. "I want to get something upstairs."

She returned in a few minutes with a small lacquered box in her hands. There was a tiny key in the small lock and when she had turned it and lifted the lid, Marian saw that the box was filled with photographs and small papers.

"Still Waters, these are my two sons," said Mrs. Neal quietly, handing Marian two faded photographs.

The pictures showed two curly-headed lads, boys of perhaps six and eight years old, dressed in quaint little suits, each smiling an embarrassed and yet friendly smile, under the ordeal of being photographed.

"I lost them—twenty years ago," Mrs. Neal said in the same curiously quiet tone. "They were—drowned."

"Oh!" cried Marian, tears springing to her eyes.

"I haven't read the letters the Common Council has been sending me," said Mrs. Neal. "Nor did I open the letters from your uncle. My lawyer wrote me the town wished to purchase some of my land, but he made no mention of the purpose. I didn't even know there was a Glory River—or that other mothers worried. My lads were drowned in a river—wading one afternoon."

Marian looked at her, the tears brimming over now. But the lady in white was not crying.

"I send the flowers from my gardens to the children's hospitals in the city," said Mrs. Neal, turning the papers over in the box. "And my knitting goes to the babies' hospitals and homes. But it seems I have neglected needs nearer home. Would you like to help me redeem myself, Still Waters?"

"Yes," said Marian without a moment's hesitation.

"Then we'll plan together now," the lady in white announced, "and you shall be my spokesman."

CHAPTER XX

APPOINTED AMBASSADOR

"ARE you going out to-night, Uncle Cornelius?" asked Marian.

They had finished dinner. If the Mayor had been watching his niece closely, he could scarcely have failed to notice her manner of subdued excitement. She started when Mrs. Carey spoke to her over her shoulder, having approached noiselessly, and she scarcely touched her food, but drank three glasses of water, a fact which Mrs. Carey did not fail to notice.

"My land, I hope you're not burning up with fever, Marian," said the housekeeper anxiously, as Marian was following her uncle out of the dining room.

"Oh, no—I'm all right," Marian returned breathlessly.

"Going out?" repeated the Mayor, in answer to her question. "No, not this evening; I expect Mr. Singleton and three or four other men here for a conference."

"Could I—could I speak to you first—I mean

before they come?" Marian asked, a bit panic-stricken at the idea of having to hurry.

She had a great deal to tell and it was imperative that the Mayor hear it before he held another conference with the Council members. She knew, without being told, that the meeting was to consider the question of the playground.

"Come into the library," said the Mayor.

He was reminded, as he seated himself at his desk and Marian took one of the huge leather upholstered chairs across from him, of a day years ago when Nancy had been in a scrape of some kind and had come to him to ask him to intercede with the school authorities. There could be no greater contrast between his memory of the vivid, gypsy-like beauty who had smiled and cried and stubbornly defied him and the mild blue-eyed girl, Nancy's daughter, who faced him now. But if Nancy Bolton had suddenly replaced Marian in the great chair the shock would hardly have been greater than the first words he heard in the pleasant, even voice to which he was unconsciously growing to like to listen.

"Mrs. Neal says she will make a gift of the playground," said Marian.

She had no flair for dramatic effects and she

made her statement as simply and as straightforwardly as she would have said that the breakfast rolls were waiting in the oven.

"Mrs. Neal said what?" the Mayor questioned in astonishment.

"She says she will make a gift of the playground—to Stillwell," repeated Marian.

"But you don't know her—she has never been outside the house since it was built for her a dozen years ago," the bewildered listener protested.

"Mrs. Neal has never seen or talked with anyone in Stillwell. She communicates with her gardeners and the tradespeople through notes left in a box on the porch. How could she make a statement of that kind to you?"

"Oh, we are friends," the pleasant voice assured him, with only a little tremor of excitement in it to show that the speaker was alive to the value of her news.

"We are friends, Uncle Cornelius. She calls me Still Waters and I have the key to her garden."

Mayor Bolton acknowledged to himself that he would never be able to puzzle it out.

"I did not know that you had ever seen Mrs. Neal or knew where she lived," he said. "Suppose you tell me all about it."

He helped her with a few questions and Marian told him the story of her friendship with the lady in white. She did not know it, but in her recital she revealed something of her loneliness, her desire for companionship and her overwhelming wish to be beautiful as her mother had been.

Before she had finished, the Councilmen arrived, and Marian, who would have liked to make her escape, found herself committed firmly to the necessary introductions. Mr. Singleton smiled warmly and said he was glad to see her again.

"I shall have to ask that my niece be admitted to our conference this evening," said the Mayor with formal seriousness. "She has a most important communication to lay before us."

Marian blushed and the visitors stared.

"It's only that Mrs. Neal is willing to give her land for a playground," she said, seeing that she was expected to speak.

An immediate flood of questions was released. Did she know Mrs. Neal? Had she talked to her? Why hadn't she answered the many communications sent to her? Was she ready to sell and when could they hold a conference with her?"

Their excitement helped Marian's composure and she found it easier to talk connectedly.

"Mrs. Neal doesn't wish to sell her land," she told them. "She is willing to give as many acres as you need—for a memorial to her two sons."

"Why—what—her sons!" gasped Mr. Goodwin, a stout and red-faced man. "How could she ever keep children out of sight—and yet we've never seen them."

"They died twenty years ago," Marian said gently. "Before Mrs. Neal had her house built and moved to Stillwell. She didn't know about the Glory River, or she might not have come here: her sons were drowned in a river."

No one spoke for a few minutes.

"And we are to understand that she offers to present the town with land for a playground, making the gift in memory of her sons?" said Mr. Singleton presently.

"Yes," nodded Marian. "Yes, that is what she said. She would like it to be called the Allan Roy Playground—her boys were named Allan and Roy—but she said to tell you that she will make the gift with no reservations, providing it is in the agreement that it is to be open all the year round and to all the children who live in Stillwell. She is going to write for catalogues to-night so she can place orders for the equipment."

"The equipment!" echoed the dazed councilmen. "Does Mrs. Neal plan to give the equipment, too?"

"Oh, yes," Marian assured them. "She said so. As many acres as you need and completely fitted up for children of all ages. I told her about the playground we had in Villyea," she added.

"You seem to have told her nothing less than magic," declared Mr. Singleton. "We've spent months trying to accomplish what you have brought about, seemingly without effort. The playground should be named for *you*."

"Oh, no," Marian disclaimed and they laughed a little at the familiar exclamation.

"And when are we to meet Mrs. Neal and make the necessary arrangements?" asked Mr. Goodwin, while the Mayor leaned back and studied his niece in silent amazement.

For the first time Marian looked a little self-conscious.

"I'm—sorry," she said gently, "but Mrs. Neal—she doesn't go out of the house, you know—she never has anyone come there—"

"You mean she is unwilling to meet the committee—is that it, Marian?" put in the Mayor crisply.

"Yes, I think so," Marian said. "Mrs. Neal told me that unless you are willing to take the gift on those terms—her terms, you know—that she will withdraw her offer. She will not meet anyone, or allow anyone to come to her house: I am to take the papers to her and she will send them to her lawyer. Everything will be quite legal, she says, only it may take a little longer than usual."

"But you're only a girl—you're not old enough to know what you are doing," sputtered the red-faced Mr. Goodwin. "I don't like an affair like this—too much mystery about it. Doesn't sound sensible. Is Mrs. Neal queer—out of her head, I mean? If she is, she can't give a deed."

"There is nothing the matter with Mrs. Neal's mentality," broke in Mr. Singleton with decision. "I know her firm of lawyers and something of her personal history. She is eccentric, to be sure—she has had trouble enough to account for that—but my advice to you is to accept her terms without quibbling. I'll bank on little Miss Blessing—she can see the matter through."

And, as it turned out, his advice was followed. There was really nothing else to do, if they wished the town to benefit by the generous offer of a completely equipped playground. Mrs. Neal was steadfast in her determination to see no one —to let no stranger through the iron gates. Marian was the one medium of communication and she found herself—much to her embarrassment—being pointed out in Stillwell as "the girl who got us the playground."

She attended staid and solemn Council meetings and explained the plans of Mrs. Neal, receiving from the members messages and papers in turn, which she carried to the lady in white. She obediently did as Mr. Singleton instructed her and aroused his admiration by the quiet, unquestioning way she followed his directions and tried to understand the dry technicalities with which the law hedges about the simplest action. The Drayton boys used to stare over the hedge as the Mayor handed her into the car and drove away with her to attend a conference or to meet the surveyors or contractors who presently were busy at the work of transforming the smiling fields into an up-to-date playground for happy children.

There was a great deal of detail to be taken care of and the refusal of Mrs. Neal to meet anyone caused almost endless complications. The manufacturers of the equipment, scenting large orders, sent their representatives to see her: the architect who was to draw up plans for the hall which was to occupy one corner and the mason who was to do the wading pool, said they must consult her: to them and to the dozens of people who were gradually connected with the project, Mrs. Neal sent the same answer: she would see no one and any communication they cared to make, might be made to her through Miss Marian Blessing, her representative.

Usually "Miss Blessing" astonished the busy and enthusiastic men who came down from the nearby cities to forward the work. They were eager men, glad to be associated with a project that was to be made as nearly ideal as money and loving purpose could make it.

"We were told to ask for Miss Blessing," a serious-eyed committee might say, rising when Marian entered the living-room into which Mrs. Carey would have shown the callers.

"I am Marian Blessing," she would answer in her pleasant, even voice.

"But—but we have brought the plans for the rest pavilion—or the game section, or the tennis courts—" a chorus would stammer.

"I know—I will look at them,"—Marian's calmness was vastly reassuring despite her youthful appearance.

And in a few sentences she would reveal to them that she not only knew "what she was talking about"—as one of them expressed it—but what they were talking about, also.

"And bless you, Marian doesn't get the least bit excited," said Mrs. Carey to Miss Hope Palmer, who was almost beside herself with curiosity —and this curiosity of the town concerning Mrs. Neal was the greatest trial with which Marian had to contend.

"She goes right on, copying notes for the Professor and sorting his clippings and having housekeeping confabs with Peter Parsons and playing with Dix. She's been making a dotted Swiss dress half the summer and she never gets a chance to finish it. As soon as she has a minute to herself, someone calls to ask her where this is to go or what they're to do with that—and the Mayor is as pleased as Punch, if you ask me. He didn't know she had it in her and he's that proud!"

And upstairs in her own room Marian, sewing on a button for the perpetually buttonless Dix, was wondering, if she should suddenly grow pretty, whether Uncle Cornelius would be proud of her and, best of all, tell her so.

"If I could only be beautiful—like my mother!" she sighed, and doubled her thread to add security to her work.

CHAPTER XXI

DAVID TUMBLES

THE kitten Marian had rescued apparently had no home and, as Mrs. Carey was willing, had been allowed to adopt the Bolton house and grounds as a permanent residence. It outgrew the starch box the second night and now roamed contentedly about the garden, sleeping wherever sleep overtook it. But it seemed doomed to misfortune and as Mrs. Carey observed, if there was anything to fall into, or get caught on, they might expect that kitten to fall into or be caught.

Perhaps it was the extra work connected with the establishment of the playground, perhaps the heat wave that descended on Stillwell and made its "cool nights" an idle boast, but Marian, as the summer advanced, did not sleep as well as usual. Sometimes she would lie awake for an hour or two, listening to the strange creaks and odd noises that can always be heard at night when the customary sounds of familiar day are hushed. Marian did not get up to investigate the noises, nor was she uneasy: she would lie quietly, thinking, and only an unusually loud snap or crack would bring her upright in bed, or send her scurrying to the window to see if anything was moving on the lawn.

"I do believe I go to bed too early," she said impatiently to herself one night when, after an hour or two of slumber she found herself wide awake and no amount of "counting sheep" would send her back to dreamland.

"Mrs. Carey says if she goes to bed too early she lies awake, but if she stays up she is so sleepy she can't keep her eyes open and she sleeps till morning. I ought to stay up till ten or eleven o'clock."

Naturally the slight difficulty to be faced was the positive objection of her uncle. Marian had a shrewd suspicion that no argument would convert him to a later bedtime for her. But what was there to hinder her staying up, once she went to her room? The Mayor very seldom came in before eleven or twelve and she would take care to have her light out by half past ten at the latest.

"Perhaps then I'd get a little sewing done," thought Marian, who found that making a dress by hand was a tedious performance, especially as she was a stickler for neatness and refused to hurry at the expense of precision.

The very next night she put her theory into practice. The Mayor went into the city on an earlier train than usual that morning, leaving word that he would have dinner at his club with Mr. Singleton and be out on one of the late trains. Mrs. Carey and Marian had dinner together and afterward sat on the porch while Mart Powers soaked grass and shrubbery with the hose, in an effort to cool the stifling atmosphere.

"There—he's flushed out that kitten," said the housekeeper in a resigned voice as with a loud and indignant "Meow," the kitten dashed from behind a rose bush and, tail erect, dashed around the house, probably to find refuge under the back porch.

Mart laughed, said something about a fur coat in this kind of weather.

"There's the nine o'clock whistle," Marian murmured. "I wonder if it is any cooler upstairs now than it was this afternoon?"

"It can't be any hotter," returned the philosophic Mrs. Carey. "And I for one, want to get out of this dress—she would make it with double collar and cuffs and I'm just about roasted."

So they turned out the lights, except the one

in the hall always left burning for the master of the house, and went upstairs together. Marian found her room warm, but a faint breeze was beginning to stir the curtains, promising an endurable night. It was out of the question to think of sewing—the very thought of a needle was distressing—and she made up her mind to read. She had to go down to the library to get the book she wanted and as she passed through the hall on her return, she heard David's voice shouting angrily. He was probably quarreling with Donald, she thought—the windows were open in both houses and the sounds carried easily. She heard Dix bark defiantly, "I won't!" then a screen door slammed sharply and the muffled sound of sobbing came to her.

"Peter's dragging Dix off to bed," translated Marian, mounting the stairs with her book. "I do think they're all rather mean to him—he can do anything he pleases, until it bothers Peter or the older boys, and then they land on him like a ton of bricks."

She sat down on the side of her bed, intending to read as she undressed. But her book was engrossing and before she had untied one shoe lace, she was lost to the world and time. The hooting of a distant screech owl broke the spell for her at last and with a start of dismay she saw that it was half past eleven.

"My goodness, have I been reading all that time?" she thought in surprise. "You don't suppose Uncle Cornelius has come in and I didn't hear him?"

But the light was burning in the hall and Marian, who did not feel at all sleepy, decided to go down and put away her book and get a drink of water. Mrs. Carey always kept a bottle of water on the ice.

Marian had her drink of water, first slipping her book into its niche on the library shelf, and then stopped a minute at the kitchen door to peer through the screen at the witchery of the night. She almost cried out as footsteps sounded a moment on the gravel walk and something shot past the door.

"David!" she gasped in a whisper. "I don't see what he can be doing, to be out late so often."

Acting on impulse, she unhooked the screen door and stepped out on the porch. She thought she would make sure it was David and by keeping her eye on the rain pipe, her guess could be substantiated. Sure enough, the bunched-up little figure appeared in a moment, silhouetted against the corner of the house, as he worked his way up the slender galvanized pipe.

"I wonder where he goes?" raced Marian's mind. "I wonder what he does!"

Alas, among the many repairs needed by the Drayton house, none was more urgent than that of new leaders. But the estimate from the plumber had so shocked Peter Parsons, that he had never even mentioned the figures to the Professor. So the leaders continued to rust and the gutters cracked and the rain water gushed from the roof in unchecked torrents during every storm.

Under these conditions what happened was not surprising. The wonder was that it had not happened long before. David was of normal weight and a rusty rain pipe in its palmiest days was never designed to serve as a stairway. As Marian watched she heard an ominous ripping sound, saw David clutch wildly at the shutter of the nearest window, and then pipe and boy crashed to the ground together.

David made no outcry and Marian sped across the lawn and scrambled over the hedge, wondering if he could be unconscious.

"David!" she whispered anxiously, bending

over the dark figure on the ground. "David, are you hurt?"

"You needn't shout," said David's familiar, sullen voice. "Do you want the whole neighborhood coming out?"

To her relief he sat up, rubbing his elbows.

"Gee, that made a racket, didn't it?" he commented. "See if you see Peter coming, will you, Marian?"

Marian listened intently, that being the only way of "seeing" in that inky darkness.

"I don't hear a thing," she reported.

"Pete sleeps on the other side of the house," grunted David, "so I don't believe I woke him up. Now how the dickens am I going to get into the house?"

He stood up and Marian knew that he had not been injured by the fall. She forebore to vex him with any more solicitous questions, but waited quietly.

"I can't use the rain pipe on the other side of the house, because Pete will be sure to poke his head out of his window," grumbled David. "And all the first floor windows and doors are locked—trust Pete to see to that."

"I—I have a key," Marian said a little diffidently.

"A key—to our house?" David asked incredulously. "Where did you get it?"

David was not intentionally rude, and even if he had been, Marian was too shaken to have attempted any reproof. She had expected to find him injured, it seemed miraculous that he had escaped with no bones broken, and she was far too greatly relieved to quarrel with him, no matter what he said.

"Why, your father gave me a key," she explained quietly. "You know if Peter goes away, even just up to the grocery store, he locks the doors. And when I have notes or clippings ready, I bring them over and leave them on the hall table for your father. I don't like to go upstairs and bother him when he is busy. And if I knock on the door—and he hears me—that interrupts him, too. So he gave me a key."

"Can you find it?" asked David.

"Find it?" Marian repeated, puzzled.

"Sure—find it. Do you know where it is?"

David was quite sincere. He never, by any chance, knew where any of his possessions were and when he most needed them an anguished search was the usual procedure. If he had had a door key and been asked to produce it, he knew he would have had to consume valuable time in hunting for it. He assumed that Marian would be in the same difficulty.

"Of course I know where it is—up in the top bureau drawer in my room," said Marian.

"Well, don't stand here all night talking," David urged ungraciously. "Go on up and get it—I can't stay out here till morning."

But as she started, he called her back.

"Say—you're not going to tell anyone you saw me, are you?" he asked hurriedly.

"Why—no, I suppose not," Marian admitted. "Why should I?"

"Promise?" said David quickly. "All you have to do is keep still and no one will ever say a word. Promise, Marian."

Marian promised half absently, her thoughts intent on securing the key. It didn't seem so important at that moment whether anyone heard of David's escapade or not—the main question was, could he get into his house without arousing the slumbering neighborhood?

Marian hurried back to the house, dashed up to her room and found the key without trouble. The necessity for moving quietly, so as not to waken Mrs. Carey, took a little more time, of course, but she was back before David expected her. His only comment was a grunt.

"Which door's it for?" he asked in an undertone.

"The front one," Marian replied, handing it to him. "The door squeaks a little, David."

"Huh, they all do that," said David, tramping through the wet grass on his way to the front door.

Marian followed him and they had an anxious moment when it seemed that the screen door was securely fastened. It proved to be merely "stuck," however, and once opened, the rest was easy. David unlocked the heavy oak door, gave the key back to Marian and with a muttered "thanks," vanished.

A broad band of light flashed over the lawn and Marian's heart skipped a beat. She had forgotten that the Mayor was coming out on the late train and that was his car going in the drive. There was only one way to get into the house—through the kitchen—for the other doors were locked. Luckily she had not left a light burning in the kitchen.

"He'll go in the front way—he always does," she thought rapidly as she heard the garage doors roll together. "I'll wait long enough for him to get in the house and go upstairs and then I can go in the kitchen way."

But as soon as she had decided to do this, another thought came to her. Suppose the Mayor made a tour of the lower floor—as he frequently did—and discovered that the kitchen door was unlocked. He would slide the bolt and she would be locked out.

"I guess I'd better try to get upstairs before he does," she thought desperately and began to run.

She gained the kitchen porch breathless, slipped into the kitchen and stepped into the brilliantly lighted pantry, where Mayor Bolton was foraging for a clean napkin.

"Why—Marian!" he greeted her in astonishment. "What are you doing up at this hour? And have you been out?"

"I—I heard a noise," Marian answered, hoping frantically that she was not to be cross-examined.

The kitten mewed plaintively and scratched with his claws on the screen door.

"That fool cat, I suppose," said the Mayor impatiently. "But haven't you been in bed at all?"

CHAPTER XXII

AN UNANSWERED QUESTION

"HAVEN'T you been to bed at all?" repeated the Mayor, adding, "it is after midnight."

Marian glanced down at her dress.

"I was reading," she confessed.

"Well, it's high time we were both asleep," her uncle replied pleasantly. "And if there are any more noises, call me and I'll do the investigating."

Marian was inclined to think there was some foundation for her theory when she fell asleep as soon as her head touched the pillow. She did not waken, either, till Mrs. Carey looked in to say that breakfast was ready.

Much to her relief, her uncle did not mention the episode of the night before. He went off as usual and Marian, taking some mending she had finished, went over to the Draytons', intending to see David.

But he was not in evidence. Dix was there, extremely cross and ready to quarrel with Peter on the slightest provocation, because he had been forbidden to touch the fallen rain pipe. Donald was constructing a wagon on the side lawn and he called to Marian to come and hold the axle, while he hammered on the wheel. Peter was placidly peeling potatoes for clam chowder, seated on the top step of the back porch.

"Where's David?" asked Marian conversationally.

"Oh, he went off right after breakfast," Donald answered. "He grubs around the river a lot—Dix is mad because he wouldn't let him go with him."

"I am not mad!" announced Dix, wholly unconscious that he was appropriating a famous line. "I wouldn't go with Dave if he asked me to!"

"That's the spirit," Peter encouraged him. "Did I or did I not tell you to KEEP AWAY FROM THAT RAIN PIPE?"

Marian giggled at the change in Peter's tone.

"I guess I can look at it," grumbled Dix.

"Why don't you want him to touch it?" Donald asked, squinting along his axle, like a veteran wagon builder.

"For the simple reason that he'll be rust from head to foot and fill his eyes up with the stuff," said Peter shortly. "I haven't forgotten how he behaved with the window screen."

"It was an old one," Donald explained to Marian. "It was all rusted out and Dix brought it down from the attic and played a tune on it with the fly batter: the wires were rusted to dust and it all flew into his eyes. Pete had to take him to Doctor Armstrong."

"But why did he want to beat it with the fly batter?" asked Marian.

"If you'll tell me the answer, I'll give you my five-dollar gold piece," Peter announced grimly. "Dix doesn't need any reasons—they clutter up his thinking apparatus."

Dix scowled and Marian hastily proposed his battleship game. This was one of the infinite variety of games played with a board and "men" and Dix always took so long before each move that his experienced family side-stepped a game whenever they could possibly manage it. Marian herself hated to spend two hours in this wise, but she could not bear to see Dix unhappy. He was lonely a great deal of the time—though he did not realize his trouble—and she knew what it was to be lonely.

That afternoon she took him with her over to the playground, now a fascinating place for small boys of mechanical bent, with the steam shovels at work and the concrete mixers busily churning. There was to be a dedication day, when the place was completed and formally turned over to the town and Mrs. Neal had said that Marian was to represent her on the program.

"I'd like to see you a few minutes in the library to-night, Marian," said her uncle as the dessert was being served at dinner.

Marian followed him into the library at the conclusion of the meal, thinking that perhaps Mr. Singleton had sent a message he wished her to deliver to Mrs. Neal.

She was quite unprepared for his first words.

"Marian," he said seriously, "I'd like you to tell me exactly what you were doing last night—when you came in and found me in the pantry."

The color flooded Marian's face.

"I was out in the yard," she said.

"Did you see anyone? Were the Drayton boys there?" the Mayor sat down at his desk and motioned her to a chair.

Marian took refuge in silence. What could she say, without breaking her promise to David!

Her uncle glanced at her averted face and went on.

"Mr. Robbins came in to see me to-day—at the

office," he said. "He was raving, stark raving mad. Another one of his cottages had been rifled and he was out there on guard himself. He says the mischief was done by a crowd of young hoodlums and he is quite positive he saw Donald and David Drayton in the crowd."

"I don't believe it," Marian declared with more than usual vigor. "Mr. Robbins could be mistaken," she added, lifting her chin.

"The boys scattered before he could seize any," the Mayor admitted. "And he lost his head entirely and fired off an old-fashioned pistol he has. Luckily he had enough sense left to fire into the air; I have no patience with these hot-headed individuals who grab a gun at the first sign of trouble. We should have had a fine row on our hands if Robbins had fired into the crowd of youngsters and wounded someone."

"I don't believe Donald would break into anyone's cottage," said Marian firmly. "Or David, either."

"They'd do it as a lark, if at all," the Mayor commented. "Of course I don't for a moment think that burglary is the motive for entering these vacant cottages; but destroying furnishings and smashing windows are serious offenses enough and I'd like to punish those who are responsible."

Marian remembered what Peter Parsons had said about Dix and his desire to play on the rusty screen with a fly batter: "Dix doesn't need any reasons—they clutter up his thinking apparatus," Peter had said. Perhaps David felt the same way—if he wanted to break into a cottage, he would not need any reasons.

"Well, Marian, you haven't answered my question yet," the Mayor reminded his niece. "What were you doing out in the dark last night? What made you run? You were panting as you came in—did anything frighten you? Did you see anyone?"

Marian set her lips in a tight line because they would tremble. She looked unhappily at the Mayor, whose own mouth was set in a harder line than usual.

"Just as I thought," he said, as she did not speak. "You have nothing to say. This morning as I went out to the garage, I noticed that the rain pipe on the Drayton house has fallen down: it was in place at dinner time last night— I noticed, because I am rather observing of such trifles. That rain pipe looked to me as though a boy might have attempted to climb up it, in an attempt to get to his bedroom undetected. A good rain pipe will stand such performances, but the Drayton pipes and leaders have led a long life and their usefulness is nearing the limit, I should say."

Marian stared at him. How could he know so much? It never occurred to her that Mayor Cornelius Bolton had grown up in a small town and that, as a lad, he had climbed the rain pipe of his father's house on more than one night when he had stayed out later than the household rules permitted.

"I won't ask you if you saw Donald and David come down with the rain pipe," pursued the Mayor, "because in your present frame of mind I doubt if I should obtain an answer. These things come to light, sooner or later, so I think for the present we'll drop the subject."

Marian looked at him appealingly, but he drew a pad of paper toward him and began to write. She was evidently dismissed.

She spent a miserable evening in her own room. During the weeks in which she had been the center of the playground conference, Marian had the feeling that she and her uncle were coming closer together. He talked freely to her, seemed glad to introduce her to the council members and his,

"Where's Marian?" when he came home from his city office sounded as though he had missed her through the day.

"Now he'll think I am mean and stubborn," thought Marian despairingly. "I just cannot tell about David— Oh, dear, I don't see why boys have to act so!"

The Mayor did not mention the matter at the breakfast table and the meal was rather a silent one. Marian made a few timid comments to which her uncle replied with scrupulous politeness. Mrs. Carey sensed that something was wrong, but she forebore to question Marian, even when the Mayor's departure for the station gave her ample opportunity. The housekeeper's innate kindness was stronger than her curiosity.

Marian was restless. She worked at the Professor's unending notes for a few minutes; took a stitch in a stocking of Donald's; nothing seemed to be worth while. She found that the dotted Swiss dress, nearly completed at last, had assumed inexplicable tendencies. It switched and twitched and refused to yield itself to her wishes.

"I guess I'll go out," said Marian aloud, putting down her needle.

But she did not want to see Mrs. Neal. She

discovered that she did not want to have to talk to anyone.

"I'll go see the river!" she decided as a sudden thought came to her.

"I've never seen the cottages or the river and it isn't so very hot this morning. I can walk out there easily."

Mrs. Carey was placidly shelling peas on the cool side porch and merely nodded when Marian paused outside the screen door to say she was going for a walk. In a way, Marian had greater freedom than any girl her age in Stillwell; though she might not have been conscious of it, she would have been happier had there been someone who cared enough to supervise her comings and goings, or to be interested in her plans.

Main Street took one to the road that wound into the "river road" and Marian had no difficulty in finding her way. The sun was excessively hot but the shade was delicious and the river road was well lined with trees. It was a long mile to the river, but when she glimpsed its silver through the leaves, Marian felt repaid for the walk.

"Glory River!" she said softly, liking the sound of the name.

Summer cottages and bungalows had been

built at irregular intervals along the banks of the river and on the other side Marian saw a jungle of vivid green and scarlet dashes that was, as she learned later, swamp and marsh land.

"I wonder which are Mr. Robbins' cottages," she thought, staring around. "Up further, I guess—people seem to be living in these nearest ones."

The signs of occupancy were unmistakable—chickens scratching lazily before one pink and green bungalow, a wash flapping on the line behind another cottage, and a tow-headed child staring silently at her from a crude pen built to keep him in the unfenced yard before a third house.

Marian saw a narrow path worn in the grass close to the river's edge and she began to follow it. Great gorgeous dragon flies darted before her and every leaf on the overhanging branches of the trees was faithfully mirrored in the glassy stream. No wonder the children of Stillwell were drawn to the river—but Marian shuddered a little as she saw how easily a small child could tumble into this silent quietly flowing water.

There was a weeping willow tree on the edge of the bank and the limbs extended out over the water. There was one long arm, Marian noted, that seemed made to tempt a climber.

"I could crawl out on that and just see how it feels," the girl said to herself. "No one will see me—I believe I'll try it."

She glanced around cautiously. The towheaded baby had evidently sat down as his head was no longer on a level with the top of his pen. There was no one in sight and Marian was sure the dragon flies would not be critical of her prowess in scrambling up the tree.

She was panting a little when she finally found herself hidden in a screen of branches and she waited a moment before she began to crawl out on the limb that hung over the water. There was something secret and thrilling about the simple adventure—Marian felt as though she might be a princess in her tower, about to pull up the drawbridge that spanned the moat.

Cautiously she edged her way along until she was out as far as she judged it safe to go. The limb swayed lightly and Marian saw her distorted reflection in the water as she held her head down to look.

"I might fish—if I had anything to fish with," she murmured lazily.

She considered the possibility of going to sleep

and tumbling off into the river, dismissed it as remote, and was just about to crawl back to land and safety when she happened to glance up stream.

"Good gracious!" she murmured, panic-stricken in an instant.

Two rowboats were slowly drifting down, each with two young couples and an array of picnic-baskets stowed dexterously in them.

"This willow tree makes a lovely shady spot," thought Marian in dismay. "Of course, they will stop here— Oh, dear, it will be awful to have to climb down before an audience!"

The boats were near enough now so that she could hear the voices of the occupants. Marian knew she ought to scramble back, but something held her from taking the first move. She did not realize it, but she was urgently hoping that the boats would drift on and put in lower down stream.

"What an adorable willow tree!" one of the girls cried out shrilly. "Billy—Fred—there's a willow tree; why can't we eat our lunch there?"

Marian automatically folded herself up in as compact a bundle as she could and regretted that her legs were so long though hitherto she had found them most serviceable for long walks.

"If I fall off and make a splash, they'll scream," she thought. "And if I stay up here and they see me, they'll think I am crazy. Perhaps they won't look up and then I can go as soon as they have rowed away."

An unaccountable shyness possessed her. It seemed the most difficult thing in the world to edge her way back to the tree, drop lightly to the ground and explain to the picnic party that she had been getting a view of the river from the branches. Marian didn't want to meet the newcomers, she didn't want to make any explanations, she didn't want to have to answer questions. So she kept perfectly still and waited for something to happen.

It did—with a suddenness that surprised the girl in the tree as much as the picnickers. Indeed it was lucky for Marian that she had presence of mind enough to grasp the tree limb with both hands as a piping treble sounded from the bank.

"Go away—you folks, git!" shrieked a very small and very dirty boy in a torn gingham suit.

"Now what's the matter with you?" one of the young men rowing the boat asked indulgently.

"You don't dast to picnic here," the small boy informed him. "This land belongs to Mr. Robbins and he won't have anyone eating on it. My father will come after you with a shotgun if you step ashore."

"How hospitable!" one of the girls giggled.

"Are you Mr. Robbins?" the other asked.

Marian, staring through the branches, saw the child's face redden in anger.

"My father takes care of Mr. Robbins' cottages and he won't have any folks eating on this land," the lad declared.

"Give him a dollar, Fred," the girl who had pointed out the willow tree suggested.

"I don't take money—Mr. Robbins pays my father," said the boy, but he looked wistfully at the handful of change the young man called Fred pulled from his pocket.

"All right, Bub, seems to me I've heard it said that this Robbins thinks he owns the rivers and the tides as well as the land," said Fred. "We won't camp out here, if you're so set against it But I'll give you a quarter if you'll tell me of a nice shady place where we *can* eat our lunch in peace."

"You go right down the river, about a quarter of a mile and you'll find a big oak—larger than this and much shadier," said the boy, evidently anxious to earn his money.

"Nobody waiting for us with a shotgun?" Fred suggested.

"Nobody owns the land," the boy responded. "You can do anything you want to—thanks, mister."

He caught the shining silver piece neatly, but he sat down cross-legged on the grass.

"Guess I'll wait till you row away," he said composedly.

The occupants of the two boats laughed, but the young men picked up their oars and began to move off. In a few minutes they were far enough away to satisfy the deputy of the caretaker and the boy rose to his feet whistling.

He gave Marian a bad five minutes while he stood apparently undecided as to what to do next. But, having admired his coin minutely, he finally slipped it in his pocket and departed toward the cottages, whistling.

Marian waited until he had disappeared and then she waited another five minutes as an extra precaution before she slid down the trunk of the tree.

"If Mr. Robbins won't allow a picnic on his grounds, he isn't likely to encourage visitors, either," she told herself, glancing around to make sure that no man with a shotgun was heading for *her*.

She saw no one, and, brushing the leaves and twigs from her skirts, resumed her walk following the river and stopping now and then to toss a stone into the placid depths.

"Now those must be the Robbins' cottages," Marian assured herself as she came in sight of four attractive bungalows with boarded-up windows.

"Wonder which is back and which is front?" mused the girl and indeed it was difficult to decide, for the architectural features gave no clue. Porches extended the full width of two sides of each house.

Marian finally decided that the front of a cottage should face the river and this knotty point settled, she left the beaten path intending to walk around and inspect the back of the bungalows.

"Hello!"—a familiar figure raised itself from the floor of the porch of the first bungalow as her footsteps sounded on the graveled path.

"Why—David!" Marian was so surprised she could think of nothing else to say, but stood staring at him dumbly.

"I suppose you've blabbed all over town about last night?" challenged David.

He had been lying flat on his stomach on the porch floor and now he was hastily stuffing something into a tin can between his knees.

"You know I haven't told—I promised you," Marian answered evenly. "But, David, do you know what people are saying? Mr. Robbins thinks you and Donald broke into one of his cottages last night."

"Huh, Robbins is an idiot—always was," said David, and his easy dismissal of the charge was more convincing than a heated protestation of his innocence.

"What would I want to bust into his cottage for?" he went on. "And old Don went to movies —saw him myself."

"Well, Uncle Cornelius heard about it," said Marian, sitting down on the porch step. "And, David—when I went in last night, he was in the pantry and saw me come in."

"He did?" David was no longer indifferent. "Did he ask you where you'd been? What did you say?"

"What could I say?" Marian returned.

David glanced at her and seemed relieved at what he read in her face.

"That's all right—you can tell him anything you want to, when two weeks are up," he assured her graciously. "Just you keep mum for the next two weeks and then you can go as far as you like. I'm working on an important scheme," he added mysteriously.

CHAPTER XXIII

THE GREAT SCHEME

DAVID evidently considered that he had made every concession that could reasonably be expected of him when he offered to release Marian from her promise within two weeks' time. That she might be placed in an uncomfortable position, or be made unhappy, because of her silence, either did not occur to him, or he thought it unimportant.

He walked home with her, from the river and left her at the hedge, without again referring to the matter. It was plain that, as far as he was concerned, the subject was closed. He had been out late, Marian had seen him, the whole disturbing question would be answered in good time.

Nearly a week passed and Marian, absorbed in the details still to be decided in connection with the playground, was still trying to convince herself that her uncle had forgotten the incident of the rain pipe, when David surprised her by seeking her out one noon.

He stood on the lawn and whistled to her, making mysterious beckoning motions with his arms and hands when she came to the screen door.

"I haven't had lunch yet," said Marian. "Mrs. Carey just called me. Is it anything important, David?"

"I'll wait," David replied, dropping down on the grass. "You go on and eat and come right out as soon as you're finished. Don't dawdle around till Don or Dix come snooping over here."

David's usually rather sullen moody face was alive with interest and Marian, as she ate her luncheon with more speed than usual, tried to imagine what it could be that he had to tell her. Surely it must be something about his night expeditions. Perhaps he was ready to let her explain to the Mayor.

She hurried out, foregoing dessert in her anxiety not to keep him waiting, and David leaped to his feet as he saw her coming.

"We'll go out to the barn," he said eagerly.

They skirted the Bolton garage and came around the Drayton barn from that angle, thus keeping out of range of Peter's kitchen windows. Marian wondered at the secrecy and more than ever when David closed the rickety barn doors as soon as they were inside.

"Sit down," he said, dragging up a soap box for her and another for himself.

Marian faced him in the dim light that came through the cobwebby windows and was more at a loss than ever to fathom what was on his mind.

"This is awfully important—what I'm going to tell you," said David very seriously. "And if you tell, or give it away before the right time comes—well, I don't suppose I could do anything, but I'd never trust you again."

Poor Marian, remembering the disastrous results of one promise, might have been pardoned a sharp retort. She merely said quietly, "You know I won't tell, David, if you ask me not to."

"Well, I don't suppose you would," conceded David. "I thought I could get along without telling anyone, but I'm stuck. I'm writing a book."

"Writing a book?" Marian echoed. "You mean a real book, like your father's?"

"What kind of a book do you suppose I'd be writing?" demanded David irritably. "Of course it's a real book—maybe it won't be as long as Dad's, but then some books are shorter than others."

Marian stared at the self-confessed author in fascination.

"Isn't it a great deal of work?" she inquired respectfully.

"Work! I should think it was!" David mopped his brow with a dingy handkerchief as though the very thought made him warm. "That's where you come in," he informed her calmly.

Marian folded her hands in her lap and waited.

"You see," said David earnestly, "I meant this book to be a surprise. Dad's birthday is August sixteenth, and I meant to have it written and give it to him. But it took me longer to collect my material than I expected and now I won't have time to write it, unless someone helps me. I want it to be plain writing and it has to be in ink. It's hard to write a book in a hurry."

"Yes, it must be," Marian agreed. "What do you want me to do, David—arrange your notes?"

"Haven't any," said the author promptly. "What I'd like you to do is to write down what I say—I can tell you everything and you write it in pen and ink. I have the book all ready and a bottle of ink and everything."

Marian had never heard of this way of producing a book, but it did not sound like an impossible scheme.

"Do you know what you want to say?" she ventured, hoping that her question was not the wrong one to put to a writer.

"Sure," said David confidently. "I've got all the bugs classified, too. I can look up their scientific names while you're lettering in the titles of the chapters and things like that."

It developed that his cherished book was to be about bugs. That, he explained, was what had taken him out nights. He had visited the swamp and marsh land and captured "specimens" and studied the habits of his captives first-hand.

"I want to make it a good book," he said, his eyes glowing. "I want it to be a real book, too—no kid affair. And I can give it to Dad for his birthday and he can keep it on the shelf with his other books. See?"

Marian saw. She saw a transformed David with all the sullenness gone from his mouth and eyes, lost in his genuine eagerness and enthusiasm. She saw that he loved his patient, bookish father, loved him enough to spend tedious hours during long hot days, and tormented, mosquito-infested hours at night, working in the swamp, in order to have something of real value to write about. She saw that this gift would truly have something of David in it and represent perseverance and sacrifice.

She saw, too, if she accepted it, a long and exacting task ahead of her. David was impatient and irritable. He would be a veritable slave driver, without meaning to be unreasonable. She had enough to do now to keep her busy. If she did this writing for him, she would have to give up something else, probably her leisure hour or so in the morning.

"You will, won't you, Marian?" David was saying anxiously. "You see, I have to get it done for Dad's birthday; and I did one page and it smudged and looked fierce. If I have to copy each one over, I won't be done before Christmas."

"All right, I'll do it," said Marian. "Where do you want to work—over at your house or in ours?"

"We have to do it in the barn," David announced. "I won't have Don or Dix snooping around; they'd tell and spoil everything. Or if they didn't, Peter would want to know what I was doing and likely as not he'd tip over my cans of specimens. He's awfully careless when he's sweeping around."

"There's the library in our house," suggested Marian. "Uncle Cornelius is gone all day and we can work there just as well as not."

"Mrs. Carey won't let me bring bugs into the

house," David objected and Marian had to admit that the housekeeper would never in the world allow a collection of dubious-looking tin cans to ornament the library table or desk.

"The barn is all right," urged David. "I know a swell place to write—upstairs in the harness-room. It has a door and everything, so we can shut it when we're not working. Come on up and look."

Marian followed him up the ladder and together they inspected the stuffy little room. There was one window, nailed down, but David promised to get a hammer and open it and then, he declared, the place would be as cool as "all outdoors." Marian had her doubts, but he was so eager to have the details settled that she finally agreed they could write up there.

"But I have to have a desk or table, don't I?" she asked helplessly.

Dix stared at the barren place disconsolately. There was nothing in it beyond a row of hooks that had once held harness.

"I don't see how we could get a table up here," he said perplexedly. "Someone would be sure to miss it and hunt for it, or else see me carrying it and want to know what I was doing."

"All right," Marian gave in, "I can write on

the floor. But you'll have to spread out clean newspapers, David; these splinters are too dangerous. When do you want to start?"

"Now," said David with a decision that boded well for his future.

Marian had intended to sew on her dress that afternoon—she thought whimsically that Effie would call the dotted Swiss "hoodooed" and certainly never had a dressmaking job dragged as that one had—but David looked so eager and anxious, she could not disappoint him.

She did insist that he get the hammer and open the window in the harness room—a detail he would have overlooked in his excitement—and she insisted on the clean newspapers. These provided, she announced that she was ready.

David had a bottle of ink—filched, she suspected, from his father's desk, and a red penholder fitted with a stub pen. He had also secured two small blotters and a large square blank book on which he had pasted a label bearing the impossible title, "The Native Bugs of Stillwater, by David Drayton."

"I suppose you'll divide it into chapters," suggested Marian, sitting cross-legged on the floor, the ink beside her, the book in her lap. "And what about titles for each chapter?"

"I'll think up the first one while you print the top line," David said.

He sat opposite her, surrounded by a small fleet of tin cans, each harboring some carefully classified form of bug life.

"The title for the first chapter is 'Bugs,' " he announced calmly, when Marian had carefully lettered in the title of the book across the top line and printed "Chapter I" beneath.

David began to dictate and the great idea took definite shape. Since the author was new to his task and his amanuensis was equally untried, it was inevitable that their first efforts were characterized by mistakes and interruptions. David had small patience with the first, but Marian never lost her temper over the second, though David thought nothing of changing whole paragraphs after they were neatly transcribed.

"I'll copy this first chapter over," said Marian, when they heard the five o'clock whistle blow and knew that they would be expected to appear in their respective homes and make some preparations for dinner.

"I think if you'll go over what you want to say in your mind first, David, you'll find it easier to tell me what you want."

"When will you write some more?" asked David, watching her cork the ink bottle.

"Well, I have to go and see Mrs. Neal in the morning," Marian said slowly, "and in the afternoon I had some mending I wanted to do."

"Aw, Marian, the sixteenth will come before I get this done if you're not careful," pleaded David. "Can't you do some more to-morrow afternoon? It won't be too hot—there's always a breeze up here."

Marian wiped her dripping face—the harness room was a small furnace—and said she would work at the book the next afternoon.

Of course, after that, she was committed. David was ruthless in his demands and seldom thanked her for the time she devoted to him. But he was pleased with the neat pages and he developed an ability to marshal his thoughts more readily which, mixed with a rather unusual command of simple English, made it easier for his faithful secretary to write as he wished. She even neglected his father's notes to help the son and without intending to, upset the even schedule of the Mayor's household.

The first of these occasions was when Mrs. Carey had gone uptown on the afternoon allotted to the meeting of the sewing circle. It happened to be a postponed meeting and fell on Monday, which meant that the laundry would call for the Mayor's shirts and collars in the housekeeper's absence.

"I'll leave the bundle on the hall table, and all you'll have to do, Marian, is to hand it to the man," said Mrs. Carey, rustling way in her best summer gown.

But Marian, busy with her secretarial duties, never knew when the laundry man called. And a few days after that lapse, she was woefully late for lunch.

"I declare, Marian, this is the second day you've been late for lunch," said Mrs. Carey on another occasion, when the book had attained a difficult chapter which had required more than the usual amount of concentration. "Can't you tell time any better than this? If there is one thing I can't stand, it's having folks late to their meals."

CHAPTER XXIV

TWO CONSPIRATORS

THE subject of meals—rather the time at which they were served—soon became a matter for heated discussion between the author and his secretary. David paid not the slightest attention to the schedule Peter Parsons operated, and if he turned up for lunch or dinner after the meal had been cleared away he managed to satisfy his appetite with something from the ice box, with or without Peter's permission.

There was nothing like this allowed in the Bolton household. As Mrs. Carey had stated, she abhorred unpunctuality and breakfast, lunch and dinner, under her régime, were served at stipulated hours, the time never varying a minute. When Marian was late for lunch, she was vigorously reminded of her tardiness and when this happened with growing frequency, Mrs. Carey began to hint that it would be her duty to "speak to" the Mayor.

"I don't see what you do," scolded Mrs. Carey.

"You say you haven't been to see Mrs. Neal and you haven't been uptown. Now, Marian, you must have been somewhere. It's perfectly plain to me that you are doing something you don't wish to have known and I wouldn't interfere if you'd come in to your meals on time. But this straggling in, anywhere from twenty minutes to half an hour late, is a little too much for a body to stand."

Marian promised to mend her ways, but she calculated without David. He was obstinate and it is to be feared selfish, where his own interests were concerned. Because he was anxious to have his book finished in time for his father's birthday, he kept at it doggedly and seemingly never thought that Marian might grow tired or need a rest. She could not neglect the lady in white or the calls upon her in connection with the fitting out of the playground, but practically every other spare moment Marian devoted to David and his book. She carried the little clock from her bedroom out to the barn in the endeavor to keep track of meal hours, but David would not countenance breaking off in the middle of a paragraph or halfway down a page. He said the ink dried different colors and he wanted his book to present a neat appearance.

"It's so hot up here, David," said Marian one afternoon, pushing the damp hair out of her weary eyes with an ink-stained finger. "Let's go out under the pear tree; Donald and Dix aren't home and no one will see us."

"We can't carry all this junk downstairs," David objected. "Besides, Peter or Mart Powers or Mrs. Carey would come snooping around. I don't see why you feel tired—you're sitting down all the time and you don't have to do any of the thinking. Where did I leave off?"

And he went on, dictating as though the question was settled, as indeed it was. There was something about David that made argument seem futile. He cared so little for other people's feelings or opinions that, after a while, they began to accept them at his valuation.

But when Marian slipped into the house fifteen minutes late for dinner one evening, she found that her uncle held ideas similar to those of Mrs. Carey's, on the topic of promptness.

It had been a warm and trying afternoon for Marian and David, who cared as little for the heat as a young salamander, had insisted on revising the latter half of a chapter already written. She had counted on having an hour to herself to bathe and change her dress, but the hands of the clock pointed to six before she could persuade David that they had done enough for that day. The growing darkness—clouds which threatened a thunderstorm—finally persuaded him. He wished for a lamp, but Marian drew the line at working by lamplight. She said she was going in and she fled.

Her uncle was already seated at the dinner table and she had to pass the dining-room door to reach the stairs. It was impossible to slip by and not be noticed.

"You're late, Marian," he called to her.

"Yes—I'm sorry—I'll be down in a minute—" she mumbled over her shoulder as she sped up the steps.

She dared not stay to change her dress, but hastily bathed her face and smoothed her hair. She knew she looked warm and untidy still, but anything was better than prolonging her absence from the table.

"I'm sorry, Uncle Cornelius," she murmured again, as she took her place.

"Mrs. Carey tells me you're growing careless about coming in to meals," said the Mayor gravely. "You look warm, Marian—where have you been?"

Marian wished, with a flash of irritation, that

she need not always be asked that question. If she said "out in the barn," David's whereabouts would also be disclosed and he had impressed it strongly on her that he didn't wish the other boys to know where he went when he disappeared. In the summer the barn was not much used and David had no desire to have it known that he spent hours there.

"I was—busy," she answered in desperation.

She was conscious of a glance of cold displeasure.

"I'm sorry to seem to interfere with any of your plans," said her uncle, carving the steak with the deft precision with which he did everything he undertook, "but I am afraid I shall have to insist that you try to conform to the ways of the household. I don't want to hear again that you have been late for luncheon and I certainly do not wish to be obliged to mention that the dinner hour is quarter past six."

Marian's cheeks were scarlet and she wished she could get away and cry. She was desperately tired and she felt that David was the one who should have been scolded. She was pretty sure he would be sitting calmly at the table in the Drayton dining-room, or perhaps the kitchen, since the five o'clock supper would be over long ago, eating bread and milk perhaps and serenely indifferent to Peter's verbal lashing. Or, if Peter refused the bread and milk, David would picnic by himself out in the barn—Marian knew where he and Donald had their canned stuff hidden. In any case, David's discipline would not be such as to affect his spirits. He refused to be downcast, and Peter always declared that it was a waste of time to punish him for what he had done—unless the Professor meted out the sentence. David's eyes would sometimes have tears in them after a talk with his father.

Mrs. Carey was rather apt to harp on a subject in which she was interested, more particularly if it was connected with something of which she disapproved, but the Mayor "said his say" and let a subject drop. Marian managed to be on time for meals the rest of the week and the book went forward satisfactorily.

"Gee, Dad's birthday will be here before we're through," announced David one muggy, moist morning several days later.

"Oh, David, I thought you had it all counted out and said you had plenty of time," Marian protested.

It was stifling in the little loft room, though the door, as usual, was propped wide open with a brick and the one small window above their heads had never been closed since David had laboriously opened it by drawing out the nails which held the frame in place.

"I did count," said David, "but I left out seven chapters. They have to go in, too," he added hastily, anticipating Marian's suggestion. "I can't leave them out—they're important."

"Well, I can't go one bit faster than I'm going," Marian informed him with more firmness than she usually displayed. "If I write too fast your father won't be able to read what I have written. And you want all the titles printed and the names of your bugs, too."

David pondered, a worried pucker between his eyes. He had had no idea that it meant so much work and trouble to write a book, and his respect for his father's efforts had trebled since beginning his own undertaking.

"If you could write all day, we could finish it in plenty of time," he suggested earnestly.

"David!" Marian surveyed him reproachfully.

"You know I have to go over to the playground every day," she said. "I have to go and see Mrs. Neal almost every day—every other day at least. Then I cannot drop the notes I am doing for your father altogether, though, as it is,

I am far behind with them. He's too good to say a word. Besides, I have other things I just have to do."

Her gaze at that moment was on a very neat patch on the elbow of David's blue galatea shirt. She had placed the patch there herself.

"You could cut out the sewing," said David, who, to do him justice, knew nothing of the mending done in his behalf.

"I never expect to finish my white dress," Marian sighed. "But that isn't the reason—I simply cannot work all day on the book, David. It is impossible."

She dipped her pen in the ink and poised it, ready. David, over her shoulder, saw where he had "left off" and began dictating. He did it with fair cleverness by this time and Marian admired the book without stint. She firmly believed it to be the work of a genius and she forgave the author all his exactions and was glad to be of help to him.

"Say," David began eagerly when the noon whistle blew and, mindful of Mrs. Carey's creamed chicken, Marian put down her pen.

"Say, Marian," drawled David.

Then he hesitated.

"I suppose you're going over to the playground this afternoon?" he suggested.

"I have to," Marian answered. "The wading pool leaks and the contractor wants me to see the tests made."

"Well, why can't you come out to-night?" said David quickly. "Come right after supper—dinner, whatever you call it. I'll be up here waiting for you and mind you don't let Dix see you. Dix is crazy to know what I'm doing and if he ever spotted you, he'd tag after you."

"I suppose I could come," Marian admitted. "Uncle Cornelius is hardly ever home. All right, David, we might be able to work an hour or two."

She kept her promise and that warm, still night, they finished two chapters before it was too dark to see longer in the harness room. The perspiration was streaming down Marian's face and David was frankly irritable, but the amount of work accomplished spurred him on to more effort.

Soon Marian was giving him each evening and, not content with the long twilight David borrowed a lantern (from Mart Powers who was blissfully ignorant of his generosity) and the two conspirators worked by lantern light till the nine o'clock whistle summoned Marian.

David never could "see" why Marian should put down her pen the instant that whistle blew, and Marian learned to be thankful for an early bedtime rule. She thought, not without justification, that David would cheerfully hold her to her task till midnight if no one protested.

"The only way to get anything done in this world," he told her one night as she held the lantern while he filled it, "is to work your head off."

"Do you think you are a genius, David?" asked Marian respectfully.

She was not poking fun at him and he did not for a moment think she could be. He put the cap back on the oil can before replying.

"Well, I'm not sure," he confided with pleasing modesty.

"What made you think of writing about bugs?" Marian demanded.

"I like them," said David, who applied that simple test to his daily life with a persistence that rendered rules and regulations powerless.

It was the next evening that the idea of full-page illustrations—in color—descended upon the author.

"Illustrations!" repeated Marian when he told her.

"Yep, illustrations—I can drug the bugs and you can do the painting because my hand shakes," said David calmly.

In vain Marian protested that she did not know anything about painting—that all bugs looked alike to her. David assured her he would mark his specimens in divisions and label them so that all she would have to do would be to fill in with the colors the letters called for.

"I have to buy something, though, and I haven't any money," said David, who could have sympathized with the financial troubles of older and more experienced writers and artists.

"What do you have to buy?" Marian inquired with some caution.

"Water color paper—a box of paints, some brushes and the right kinds of pen and ink," enumerated David, apparently overlooking his use of the singular "something."

"I can lend you the money," Marian offered, relieved that no greater outlay was required. "Can you buy the stuff in Stillwell?"

"Uptown, next the drugstore," said David. "You go do it, won't you, Marian? I hate to go in a store—they always ask you such silly questions."

Marian consented to be his shopping agent and she cheerfully purchased the items on the list as David had given them to her. She had to make two extra trips before he was satisfied—one to get thumb tacks and one to get a finer brush, but at length the author-artist thought he could begin to draw.

"You'll have to work by yourself to-night," he told her when he had laboriously sketched in the outlines for his "frontispiece."

"I'm going after more specimens, but you can copy the last two pages of that chapter and color these for me."

Marian thought it was time to assert herself.

"I can't paint at night, David," she said earnestly. "It is impossible to tell one color from another. My father never painted at night."

David plainly thought her unreasonable—and yet as the daughter of an illustrator and painter, she might know what she was talking about.

"I don't see anything to hinder you when you have the lantern," he grumbled, "but perhaps you'd better paint afternoons. I wouldn't want you to spoil any of these pictures. At any rate, you can write at night."

So Marian toiled away wearily, sometimes with David, sometimes alone, when he went off to catch a fresh supply of "specimens."

The illustrations were highly technical and David was a great stickler for the proper colors in the proper place. He knew the exact shading of every bug and Marian did, too, long before she had finished filling in his outlines. Still, she had to admit the drawings added to the attractiveness of the book.

"You ought to have a cover design," she said once, in an unguarded moment.

That was enough for David. He demanded a cover for his book and Marian, in the few spare moments she had left, painted and lettered an effective cover for him, using brown burlap and buttonhole stitching the edges to make them secure.

David was pleased—she could tell by the way he handled the cover and the number of times she found him looking at it. All he said was, "That isn't so bad."

Things went on like this and the book grew in neatly written pages steadily. Marian sometimes wondered that no one asked her where she was or what she was doing. But she was only thankful that she had to meet no comments.

Mrs. Carey supposed the girl to be somewhere in the neighborhood and as the Mayor only objected to his niece making engagements for the evening and as she was always in by nine o'clock, the housekeeper raised no question. But it was inevitable that something should happen to interrupt such a schedule.

After a trying afternoon at the playground —there were times when it was extremely difficult to convey Mrs. Neal's wishes to the contractors and workmen and when Marian found it a thankless task to be the medium of communication between strong-willed artisans and an eccentric woman—Marian came home to find that her uncle had telephoned he would not be home to dinner.

"Then he won't be out till the late train," said Marian to herself as she sat down to a solitary dinner. "I'm going to stay up late for once and help David. We can finish that long chapter with all the bug names in it and I can print each one on a separate line. I don't care if I do stay up after nine o'clock—I'll tell Uncle Cornelius myself to-morrow and take a scolding."

She was intensely interested in the book by this time and as eager as David to see it completed in time for the Professor's birthday. Then, too, the necessity for keeping it a secret, added excitement to the task and Marian rather enjoyed outwitting Donald and Dix, who were much mystified at her long absences from the side porch where they had hitherto been able to find her when she was home.

She and David worked steadily, the lantern sputtering and a cloud of moths, mosquitoes and other winged creatures attracted by the light, swarming around them, till the long chapter was finished.

"I'll have to go in," said Marian, opening and closing her cramped fingers. "Leave the book open like that till it dries, David. I wonder if it is late?"

CHAPTER XXV

IN DISGRACE

THE kitchen screen door was hooked!

Marian's first feeling of dismay, as she tried in vain to open it, turned to alarm as she considered that the front door was likely to be locked and she would have to wait on the steps for the Mayor to come and let her in. There was not the slightest chance that she could waken Mrs. Carey by ringing the bell, at least not before the entire neighborhood had been aroused; the housekeeper often boasted that, once she was asleep, nothing short of an earthquake could rouse *her*.

David had disappeared into his own house, so there was no use appealing to him to climb into a window and unfasten the door. Marian seriously thought of trying the window route herself, but the windows nearest the ground were surrounded by heavy shrubbery and she had no idea that she could unfasten one, even if she made the sill safely.

"Perhaps Mrs. Carey didn't lock the front

door," she thought in desperation, and went around to the front of the house.

The hall was brilliantly lighted and the inner door stood open. Through the screen Marian saw her uncle standing in the hall, talking earnestly to Mr. Singleton. He had not waited for the late train—and as she stepped into the path of light that streamed across the porch floor, Marian was acutely conscious of her disheveled appearance.

Her frock was wrinkled and soiled from contact with the loft-room floor. She had torn her stocking as she came down the ladder. Her shoes were covered thickly with dust and her hair was roughened and her face sure to be streaked with perspiration and dirt.

For a moment she thought of keeping out of sight until the lawyer had gone, but she had not acted quickly enough. The Mayor had heard the slight scraping sound her feet made as she stepped on the porch and now he saw her.

"Oh, dear, why did Mr. Singleton have to be here?" sighed Marian as she silently stepped into the hall, her uncle holding open the screen door for her to pass through and looking sufficiently grim to make a much more reckless girl than Marian thoroughly uneasy.

"How do you do, my dear?" said the lawyer pleasantly, apparently seeing nothing wrong. "I've been waiting to have another little talk with you, but it is so late now, I'm afraid we'll have to postpone it."

"I'm sorry," Marian murmured uncomfortably.

"Well, we make a good many demands on your time," said Mr. Singleton, patting her hand kindly, "and it isn't to be wondered at that you feel like having an hour or two to yourself now and then. I meant to ask you about the plans for the dedication ceremonies, but there is nothing that will not keep. I'll be out again some evening this week."

Mayor Bolton had said nothing, but as he followed his guest out to the car standing in the driveway, he glanced at Marian.

"I want to speak to you," he said over his shoulder.

Marian sat down in a chair drawn up before the fireplace, where a huge bunch of marigolds filled the space between the andirons. The light from the hall fell dimly across her mother's picture. In the shadows, the lovely mouth seemed to be smiling tenderly.

"Marian?"—the Mayor had come in and was looking in the library across the hall for her.

"Here I am," said Marian a little shakily.

He crossed the hall quickly and switched on the floor lamp, seating himself on the other side of the fireplace.

"Mr. Singleton waited two hours to see you to-night, Marian," he began quietly. "Mrs. Carey did not know where you were and none of us could find you."

Marian was always at a disadvantage in a situation like this. She had not the kind of temper that flames up and makes a defense of anger. She could not argue or even promise to explain later. All she could do was to retreat into herself, grow white and silent and, making a bad impression, convince the Mayor that she was obstinate and sulky.

"I've been lenient up to this point," he went on, "but when I find that instead of going to bed at nine o'clock, you are roaming around till half-past ten or eleven and have no explanation to make, I think the time for leniency is past. I came out on the 7.30 train and you were nowhere to be found; what do you suppose Mr. Singleton thinks of such a performance?"

Marian said nothing. Her hands were tightly clinched in her lap.

"And your appearance is disgraceful," said the Mayor sternly. "You look as though you had been playing tag or tumbling around in a hay mow. A girl who is careless about her personal appearance has at least one serious fault; I hope you are not going to grow up into a slovenly woman, Marian."

"I—I don't always look this way," Marian answered in a low voice.

"I want to know where you were and what you were doing," said her uncle, paying no attention to this. "Where have you been since dinner time?"

"It's a secret," Marian replied hopelessly. "I can't tell you, Uncle Cornelius, truly, I can't."

"Certainly you can," said the Mayor firmly. "You can tell me exactly what it is you are doing that keeps you out of the house till this hour at night. I suppose it is the same interest that has been making you late to meals. Not only can you tell me, but I expect you to do so."

If he had been otherwise than cold and self-contained, Marian might have yielded. A little love and patience and above all, a gentle manner, would have broken down her resistance. She was desperately tired and a kinder judge could easily have persuaded her that her confidence would be respected and that David's secret would be safe with him.

Unfortunately, Mayor Bolton was accustomed to speaking with force and authority. Under his severity was strong anxiety and a real affection for the daughter of his sister, but he believed he was in duty bound to gain an accounting from Marian as to how she spent her time and he knew only one method—sternness.

"I can't tell you," said Marian again, "truly I can't."

"Then you'll have to stay in your room tomorrow and think it over," the Mayor announced. "I can't have anything like this, Marian, and you might as well make up your mind to submit. You'll have to stay in your room until you are ready to tell me what I have a right to know."

He sent her to bed then and she cried herself to sleep. She slept later than usual the next morning and when she woke up and remembered that she was to be virtually a prisoner in her room for the day, the tears came again. But she was dressed as usual when Mrs. Carey knocked on the door and brought in her breakfast.

The housekeeper's face was an odd mixture of curiosity and disapproval, but she had evidently had her instructions from the Mayor.

"Your uncle said not to talk to you," she announced, putting the tray down on the bureau top. "When you're through, leave it out in the hall and I'll get it when I come up to do the beds."

Whatever her feelings toward the culprit, Mrs. Carey had seen to it that she had a bountiful breakfast. Marian was surprised to find she was hungry and she ate heartily. And then, her spirits rising, she began to see possibilities in a long day when no outside demands could be made upon her.

The enforced quiet was really good for her and as the hours wore away, Marian sewed on her neglected dress and wondered what David would say when he discovered that there could be no work on the book for at least twenty-four hours. She heard him asking Mrs. Carey, "Where's Marian?" once or twice and later, peering through the screen, saw him going toward the barn. Perhaps he would write a chapter or two himself, she thought, and, in the task, discover that not all the labor of book-making lies in the thinking what to write.

Mrs. Carey brought her up an excellent luncheon, but stalked in and out of the room silently. However, by dinner time she was ready to disregard the Mayor's orders to the extent of giving a kindly-meant warning.

"You know, Marian," she said, eying the tray carefully to make sure she had forgotten nothing, "the big Sunday school picnic is to-morrow. I've done nothing all day but make cake and cut sandwiches; we have the nicest time every year and I was counting on having you go and really have a good old-fashioned picnic time with all the other boys and girls."

She paused and looked at Marian uneasily.

"I suppose you mean Uncle Cornelius won't let me go, unless—unless—" Marian paused, too.

She had been looking forward to this picnic for several weeks. The Drayton boys had told her about this annual affair, to which practically the entire population of Stillwell turned out. The most wonderful luncheons were packed and there were boats on the river and races and games. Usually no one went home for supper but stayed for a gypsy meal cooked over a huge camp fire and then, when the moon came up, there was singing and story-telling to end the long, happy day.

The picnic was held under the auspices of the four Stillwell churches and as Dix had frequently and enthusiastically assured Marian, "everybody" went.

"Mr. Singleton telephoned your uncle he expects both of you to go in his car," said Mrs. Carey and departed precipitately.

Marian had not thought that Dix's "everybody" was so sweepingly inclusive. She could not vision her precise and formal uncle attending a picnic, but she learned that he was going when she went down to the library that evening in answer to his summons.

There was an unhappy half hour in store for her and before it was over the Mayor had lost his temper and Marian was crying bitterly. No amount of argument could confuse her reasoning —until David gave the word, she could not tell about the book. She held fast to this line of thought and the strength of her obstinacy surprised the Mayor, who remembered past scenes with Nancy Bolton. She had stormed back at him, stamped her pretty foot on the floor and flatly defied him, times without number; her daughter sat, a woe begone little figure, in the depths of the large chair, her blue eyes frightened and tears running down her cheeks. But that small, white face was resolute and the Mayor discovered that though silent, the will opposing his was as strong as that he had associated with the tempestuous Nancy.

"Very well," he said finally. "I see you are determined to make an issue of this thing. I hope you will be willing to listen to reason before I am forced to take drastic measures. Of course you will stay home to-morrow from the picnic. I shall not ask you to stay in your room, for you probably need regular exercise. That is all."

Marian slipped out on the porch to let the night air cool her hot face. She did not care about the picnic, she told herself desolately. She couldn't possibly enjoy a picnic when she was so unhappy.

"Marian—hey, Marian?" whispered a voice and David approached cautiously.

"What are you crawling like that for?" Marian demanded with as much irritation as she ever showed.

Her nerves were on edge and she did not feel very kindly disposed toward David at that moment.

"Well—I thought perhaps Mayor Bolton would yell at me," explained David, straightening up, but keeping his voice low as a precaution. "Dix says he is mad and won't let you go to the picnic to-morrow."

"He wants me to tell him where I was last night," explained Marian. "Mr. Singleton was here when I got home, David—and Uncle Cornelius says I have been late to meals several times and he wants to know what I am doing."

"Well, after the sixteenth, you can tell him," David declared composedly. "And say, Marian, if you're not going to-morrow, can't you work on the book? It's 'most done and I've made a lot of notes to-day; I didn't know where you were, till Mrs. Carey said you were in your room. Say, Marian, will you write some to-morrow? To kind of make up for lost time, you know?"

Marian stared at him a little queerly, but the darkness hid her expression.

"I suppose I might as well," she said quietly.

CHAPTER XXVI

THE END OF THE BOOK

THE household was early astir the next morning, for, like all well-regulated picnics, this one was scheduled for an early start. Marian found that she was expected to come to the breakfast table as usual and after the strained, unhappy meal was finished, she slipped out to the kitchen and helped Mrs. Carey with her last-minute preparations.

"I'm leaving something of everything I've cooked for you, Marian," said the good woman, who was genuinely sorry to see anyone deprived of a pleasure. "If I do say it, I think my sandwich filling is better this year than it's ever been. I packed four good big boxes, too, and no wonder my feet are killing me before it's time to start.

"I put up a lunch for the Mayor and for Mr. Singleton," rambled on Mrs. Carey, "and a box for Mart Powers and a good big box for Peter Parsons and the Drayton boys—they always carry some truck, but my land, you can't expect any man to put up a decent lunch. Peter always forgets the butter or the salt and one year he left the boiled eggs home on the table. Then, of course, I fixed a box for Hope Palmer and me —we always eat together. You'll find everything for your lunch in the ice box and I'm sure I wish you were going along with us.

"Not that I altogether blame Mayor Bolton, you understand," she said a little later to Miss Hope Palmer as the two friends were bowling comfortably toward the picnic grounds in one of the big cars Mr. Singleton had loaned for the occasion. "Children get out of hand, if you don't look after 'em, but I think Cornelius Bolton makes a mistake when he uses his courtroom manner for Marian; the whole thing is this, Hope —he wasn't severe enough with Nancy and he thinks he can avoid the mistakes he made with her by being stern with Marian. And any woman could tell him there never was two girls less alike; I declare if I didn't know they were mother and daughter, I'd be inclined to wonder if Marian could be related to Nancy."

Marian had watched the fun and excitement wistfully from the window of her room. Her uncle had insisted that she come and speak to Mr. Singleton, but the meeting had not been embarrassing, though the lawyer must have suspected something when he heard that she was not to attend the picnic.

Staid Euclid Avenue became for half an hour a lively thoroughfare, with large and small motor cars honking joyous horns before selected houses and boys and girls dashing across the lawns, calling out last-minute changes in plans. Anxious mothers shrieked directions about the lunch boxes and rescued toddling babies from under wheels that possessed an unaccountable fascination for little brains. Everyone was very busy and very happy—and Marian felt that she must be the one person in Stillwell who was deprived of the enjoyment.

She waved to Mrs. Carey and Miss Palmer—the Mayor and Mr. Singleton had left first—and then to the Drayton boys as they tumbled pell-mell into a bus with Peter and the Professor (who would have preferred to stay at home, but had promised David to go) bringing up the rear. David made a few mysterious passes with his hands, which Marian interpreted as requests to do some work on the precious book. She nodded and David, as though his responsibility was removed, fell to pummeling Dix who yelped shrilly. The bus shot around the corner and gradually the Avenue settled into its usual stillness.

Marian turned disconsolately from the window. There was nothing that she really wanted to do, she thought. She was tired of the silly, dotted Swiss dress and still more weary of David's book. She didn't want to read and she didn't want to do anything helpful, like copying notes for the Professor or mending for the boys. What she did want, she told the little friendly-faced clock almost passionately, was a little fun.

"Everyone else is having a good time," she thought, going slowly downstairs. "I wish I knew something I could do."

But any festive plans she might devise called for a companion and presently Marian decided to go and see the lady in white. There might be some new ideas for the playground, ready now in a week or so for the dedication ceremonies.

The beautiful gardens bloomed brilliantly in the midsummer sunshine and the almost uncanny stillness was unbroken even by a bird call. Marian, closing the iron gate carefully as usual, stopped under the casement windows and listened. No charming voice called to her. Well—she had wanted to talk to Mrs. Neal, but evidently it was one of the days when the lady in white cared to see no one. There was a little cocked note in the box on the back porch, however, in the box into which Mrs. Neal dropped her communications to the gardeners and the tradespeople. It was addressed characteristically to "Still Waters." So far as Marian could remember, Mrs. Neal had never used her given name.

"Dear Still Waters," ran the few lines and the date was that morning. "This is a hard day for me and I cannot talk even to you. By to-morrow I shall be more reasonable. It is twenty-one years ago to-day since I lost my Roy and Allen."

There was no signature and none was needed. Marian went quietly out of the garden and slowly home. After all, she might as well work on David's book. It would be wonderful if she could finish it for him.

She found his badly scrawled notes in the soap box they used as a desk drawer and the precious book under the brick which served alternately as a door prop and as a press to keep the pages of the manuscript flat. Marian intended to place the brick against the door, but stopped to glance over David's efforts and when a breeze slammed the door shut with a sharp report, she jumped nervously.

"I only hope I get his meaning right," she

sighed a little anxiously. "David is so fussy and if I write down the wrong thing in ink, it is too late to change it."

She dipped her pen in the ink and began to write steadily. It was characteristic of Marian that whatever she undertook to do, absorbed her thoroughly. She was not conscious of time, or of her cramped position on the floor and only when her fingers began to ache intolerably did she realize that she had hardly made a pause to rest her muscles.

"My goodness, but it's warm in here," she murmured, straightening up and glancing at the neat page she had just finished, with pardonable pride.

"I'd better open the door and that will make it cooler. And perhaps I'd better stop a while and have lunch."

She remembered Mrs. Carey's assurance that "some of everything" was in the ice box. An extra good luncheon appealed very strongly to Marian at that moment, for her breakfast had been eaten hurriedly and not under the pleasantest conditions.

She put away the ink and pen carefully, propped open the book so that the page would

dry and reached up to turn the knob of the door.
There was no knob there!

A little startled, Marian scrambled hastily to her feet. What could have become of the door knob? She had never really examined the door before, David always opening it and attending to closing it. Now as she looked closely, she saw that it was perfectly smooth—knob and lock and catch were all on the *other* side. She remembered the little black hook that David pressed back when he wanted to open the door—she recalled that he had always propped the brick against the door as soon as he swung it back—it was a spring lock and there was no way she could hope to open that door from the inside. It had locked when the breeze had blown it shut.

Marian was not frightened—she was a prisoner, but she was a prisoner in a familiar place. Someone would come and let her out presently. Only she was so hungry and she wanted that picnic lunch—and then the realization swept over her that there was no one to come and let her out. Everyone had gone to the picnic, and while someone might come at supper time, the chances were that it would be nine or ten o'clock before any of the merry-makers returned.

Marian glanced hopelessly at the window. She could not reach it—David had taken the loft ladder when he climbed up to take out the nails. There was no use in shouting, for there would be no one to hear her. The Drayton house was absolutely empty and so was her uncle's house.

"I wouldn't mind," said Marian seriously, staring straight at a crack in the wall, "I wouldn't mind one little bit if it wasn't so hot in here—and if I wasn't so hungry."

She rattled the door once or twice and examined it even more carefully, hoping to find some way of opening it, but without success. It was growing warmer, for the loft room was now receiving the benefit of the full rays of the sun. To her hunger, thirst was added and Marian had tantalizing visions of iced lemonade which Mrs. Carey frequently made for lunch on warm days.

"If I can't get out," thought the little prisoner in a brave attempt to be philosophical, "I might as well work on the book. It looks as though I would finish it, because I can't do anything else."

She sat down on the floor again and began to write. The long hot afternoon wore away. A large blue-bottle fly buzzed around her maddeningly and a sparrow came and sat on the window sill to stare inquisitively. Marian was frankly afraid of mice and when a very tiny, bright-eyed one came out from some hidden cranny and tried to find out what she was doing, she very nearly shrieked aloud. She would certainly have climbed up anywhere, "to get away from the floor" as she explained later to David, but there was no place to climb. So she pounded on the wall with the useful brick—not for worlds would she have thrown the brick at the mouse and perhaps mashed him—and the little creature went away. He returned at intervals during the afternoon and Marian eventually took to pounding with the brick quite automatically, while waiting for ink to dry, or even as she wrote with one hand and pounded with the other.

As nearly as she could tell, it was five o'clock when she was able to write "Finis" with a beautiful flourish across the lower half of the last page. Her fingers were cramped and tired and her eyes hurt, she was warm and hungry and terribly thirsty, but it was impossible not to feel a glow of satisfaction. She had stuck to the task until it was done.

But as the shadows began to lengthen, something akin to panic descended upon her. She feared a visit from the small mouse and probably a whole tribe of his relatives and friends. She might have to spend the night in this room—the thought of that was intolerable. No one would know where to look for her—and David would not be likely to suggest the barn. She knew him well enough to know that he would protect the secret of his precious book, no matter whom he sacrificed in the effort. It might be morning before anyone came—and she couldn't shout in the dead of night and arouse the neighborhood.

"Oh, dear," sobbed Marian, the tears having their way at last, "I wish I'd never seen David's silly old book!"

She mopped her eyes presently and endeavored conscientiously to find some consolation in her uncomfortable position. It was not, she assured herself, as though she had been locked in a cellar—that would undoubtedly be damp and there might be snails.

"Or if I were in the tower room, at the top of a castle, no one might ever find me," she thought dolefully. "Now I can at least make folks hear me, if I have to wait till morning to do my shouting."

It grew darker and darker and presently, in spite of her efforts to stay awake, her head nodded. She tried sitting huddled on the soap box, as a precaution against marauding mice, but found she toppled off when drowsiness overcame her. At last she gave up and, using the book as a pillow, went fast asleep on the rough boards of the floor.

How long she slept she did not know. A dazzling light woke her and she blinked, trying to escape the long rays by closing her eyes again.

"Shade that lantern, you idiot!" she heard Donald Drayton say savagely and then someone gathered her up in strong arms.

"Thank Heaven, my dear child, I've found you!" said Mayor Bolton, holding his niece close to him as though he had found something very precious indeed.

"Aren't you hungry, Marian?" piped Dix. "You didn't eat your lunch."

CHAPTER XXVII

DEDICATION DAY

MARIAN'S impressions for the next half hour were blurred and confused. She was vaguely aware that the loft room was crowded and in the circle of faces thrown into wavering relief by the flickering lantern light, she saw David, sullen and frowning, Dix and Donald, alive with curiosity, Mrs. Carey—Mr. Singleton—why, they were all there. She tried to sit up.

"Just a minute—easy—wait," said her uncle's voice.

"You can't carry her down the ladder," Dix was arguing, Dix who was never held back by the convention that older people usually have the right of way on the conversational track.

"I can if it's necessary," the Mayor shot back, but Marian was not minded to be carried.

"I'm all right," she protested. "There's nothing the matter with me."

"Aren't you faint-like?" Mrs. Carey asked anxiously.

Marian laughed and that was the most satisfactory answer she could have made. Even David looked relieved at the sound.

"I was asleep, I guess," said Marian, and now she managed to slip to the floor, although the Mayor kept a steadying hand on her arm. "Is it late? Is the picnic over—did you have a good time?"

"Give her something to eat," Peter Parsons growled. "Time enough to be answering and asking questions when the child has had a good meal. Why, if she has been up here since morning, she must be starved!"

It was David who carried the lantern and now he stood at the head of the loft ladder and held the light high while one by one they laboriously climbed down. The Mayor and Marian went first, for he seemed unwilling to let her out of his sight. Mrs. Carey was sure she would fall, but didn't, and the near-sighted Professor was only saved from stepping from the mow to the floor, without recourse to the ladder, by the watchfulness of Donald who grasped him by the coat-tails just in time.

Finally everyone was down safely and they all trooped into the house where Mrs. Carey hastily assembled a bountiful supper for Marian. Dix was the only one who had returned from the picnic hungry and he found that he could keep Marian company—as Peter observed, hunger was a chronic disease with Dix.

The Mayor was anxious for Marian to eat and not to talk, but as was only natural, she was eager to learn how they had found her. To her astonishment the hall clock struck eleven as she sat down to the table—the picnic party must have been searching for her some time before they thought of the barn.

"I thought you knew that was a spring lock," said David, who sat behind her.

He spoke in an undertone, but Donald heard.

"You ought to give up thinking," he said unkindly. "A nice mess you got Marian in—and you weren't even going to tell till I made you."

"That will do, Donald," said his father. "We won't have any quarreling. But Marian, my dear, whatever took you to the loft on such a warm day?"

Marian hesitated. She saw her uncle's eyes fixed on her curiously. Mrs. Carey, too, was staring. Unconsciously Marian's eyes turned to David and, across the table, Donald sat suddenly erect.

"It's about time you did some talking, David,"

he announced savagely. "I'm sick of this—either you tell what you told me or I will. No, I won't keep still—and you needn't twit me with telling tales, either—you come out in the open and talk right now, or I'll do it for you."

The two boys locked glances, but David looked away first.

"You needn't make a mystery of it," he said disdainfully. "Marian was helping me write a book. It was to be a surprise for you, Dad," he explained, turning to his father and the angry tears rushed to his eyes.

"I might have known you can't keep a secret in this town," he scolded. "Marian was writing it for me and we wanted to get it done in time for August sixteenth."

"It's done," Marian assured him. "I finished it this afternoon. Your notes were wonderful, David."

"But now it isn't a surprise," objected David.

"Why, yes, it is, David," the Professor corrected. "Every word in it will be a surprise; but I am afraid you've forgotten to be fair to Marian in your eagerness to please me. We'll talk about that later."

Mayor Bolton was reserving his thoughts for later expression, too, and Marian was surprised to hear him announce the next morning that he was not going into the city that day.

"Suppose you and I go for a little drive, Marian," he suggested.

"Well—but Mrs. Neal may want me," Marian hesitated.

"She may and Dave Drayton may need you and for all I know Dix hasn't a darned sock to his name," said the Mayor. "But though the Professor may be waiting on the front porch for the last set of notes and clippings you are doing for him, you and I will go for a drive. Asking you was a mere formality—I neglected to mention that it is all settled and Mart is backing the car out now."

Marian laughed, a little bubbling laugh that made Mrs. Carey look up from the dining-room table where she was clearing away the breakfast dishes.

"I declare, I don't know when I've heard her laugh that way," the housekeeper thought. "Her mother had that trick—wouldn't it be funny if Marian was to take after her mother at this late date?"

They were out on one of the many beautiful country roads that were easily accessible from

Stillwell, before Marian thought to ask the question she had stored up in her mind.

"Uncle Cornelius, how did you know about the—the mending?" she asked, a little shyly.

"And the notes and all the rest of the odd jobs you've been burdened with all summer?" suggested the Mayor. "Yes, of course, I knew of the notes—Fred is so conscientious he wouldn't let you do work for him unless he thought I knew and approved; but I assumed you had finished them long ago. I had no idea it was a permanent assignment.

"As for the mending, Peter's conscience gave him a twinge. We had rather a heart-to-heart talk before you came down this morning. Did it ever occur to you, Marian, that you are too ready to do for other folk—that you may be imposed upon, unless you are more ready to assert your own interests?"

"No," said Marian quietly. "I *love* to sew on buttons and things for the boys and I like to help the Professor and David. David's book is truly wonderful, Uncle Cornelius."

The Mayor glanced at the serene blue eyes and smiled a little. Then he reached over and patted one of the small hands folded so placidly—

Marian never used her hands to illustrate her conversation.

"All right, Still Waters," he said suddenly.

He knew, too, it seemed, who had broken into the cottages.

"Not David?" said Marian a little fearfully, when she heard this.

"No, not David—not any of the Stillwell boys," the Mayor assured her.

"Mr. Robbins camped out there for several nights without results, but early yesterday morning, he heard someone tampering with the lock on the cottage in which he had secreted himself. He stole downstairs and managed to trap the culprits in the cellar—they proved to be three young fellows from a bungalow colony further up the river—seems they have been considering this sort of mischief purely in the light of a lark. I'm afraid they will find it much more serious before they are through with the consequences."

Before the drive was over—and they had lunch at a smart little inn, forty miles from home and barely got back in time for dinner—Marian discovered that someone had told the Mayor a good many things. He seemed to know about the demands the playground made on her time and all about David and her promises to him that had placed her in such unhappy situations; he knew that she had been lonely and craved friends. He even knew of the white, dotted Swiss dress. And, most marvelous of all, of her desire to be like her lovely mother. Mrs. Carey had been loquacious, but it was Peter Parsons, who to a naturally keen observation had added a real affection for Marian, who had been most enlightening.

On the way home, the Mayor dropped a little roll of bills into Marian's lap.

"For clothes," he said. "You'll need something for the dedication celebration. We have definitely fixed the date for August sixteenth."

"I have enough," Marian answered quickly. "I've saved almost all my allowance. I meant to get white kid pumps—and some beads—"

"Mrs. Armstrong will go into the city with you and help you get whatever you wish," said the Mayor with such finality that his niece subsided contentedly into a dream in which white frocks and blue beads and pumps with three straps—like Lelia Mason's—were blissfully mingled.

So it happened that when the important date came round, Marian was ready. Mrs. Armstrong with unerring taste had helped her choose a filmy white dress that fell in graceful folds and managed to be fluffy without fluttering ends streaming in the breeze, and which draped Marian's slight figure softly without impeding her lithe, quick step. The coveted white pumps —her first pair of white silk stockings ("actually her first," said Lelia, who had come to visit her cousin for this important occasion) and a lovely broad-brimmed, white hat completed her simple costume. The blue beads, a single chain, brought out the blue of her eyes and gave a charming touch of color.

"Why, my dear, you are absolutely lovely!" said the lady in white, when Marian unlocked the iron gate the morning of the great day and slipped in to see the donor of the finest gift Stillwell had ever received—ever would receive, the state papers, which were giving columns of space to the story, said enthusiastically.

Mrs. Neal had steadfastly refused to step beyond her threshold and it had long ago been settled that Marian was to represent her at the ceremonies. Mayor Bolton was to receive the playground for the borough and Mr. Singleton had announced that a dinner would follow the ceremonies, to be held in the playground and to which the entire town was invited.

Marian, in her white frock, stayed with Mrs. Neal till her uncle's car came for her. They were to have lunch at home and at two o'clock in the afternoon the program was scheduled to start.

"I'll remember everything and tell you everything," whispered Marian as she kissed the lady in white and ran out to find the car heaped with flowers freshly cut from the wonderful gardens.

The Mayor, looking very handsome and soldierly, beamed at her throughout luncheon and once he said, "Proud of you, Marian," when she happened to glance up and saw his intent look.

There was one thing she wanted to do before the afternoon really began. The opportunity came when the Mayor was called to the telephone, just as lunch was over.

Marian slipped into the living room and stood before the glowing portrait of Nancy Bolton.

"Do you think I am lovely, Mother?" she asked softly.

The pansy eyes smiled at her, the beautiful, parted lips seemed to be smiling.

"Marian! It's quarter of two," called Mrs. Carey, hurrying through the hall, and Marian hastened out to the porch to find the three Drayton boys watching to see her off.

"I gave Dad the book this morning and he thinks it is great," said David in a quick aside. "We're going to be at your table to-night at the dinner—Mr. Singleton said so."

The playground presented a scene of rich and riotous confusion. Strings of automobiles were already parked for blocks surrounding it when the Mayor's car entered the sweeping driveway.

"Just a minute—" someone jumped on the running board— "how about a picture, Mayor Bolton?"

Marian stared, Mr. Singleton frowned and His Honor laughed.

"Take a panorama," he suggested.

"Oh, we're going to—Abbott is attending to that," the young man on the running board said capably. "And we've got men planted at all the good spots for the speech-makers. They're taking movies too. But we want a close-up of your niece."

"I don't think that is necessary," said the Mayor rather stiffly. "As long as Mrs. Neal's picture is not appearing, I see no need for photographing my niece."

"Have to have it—and a story," the young man replied quite as firmly.

He had friendly eyes and a nice smile and

Marian found herself hoping he might have his way—whatever it was he wanted.

But when the Mayor introduced him as one Richard Groves and she found that he was a reporter and wanted to ask her questions and take her picture, Marian was dismayed.

"If you'll let me take one snap of you, I'll get the story as we go round," Groves suggested, noticing her confusion. "Hey, Gaspard—hurry up with that camera."

Gaspard, red-haired and freckled-faced, came running up, dripping with perspiration and carrying a heavy camera.

Marian, at his direction, stood quietly beside a young willow tree and in a very few moments, with no fuss at all and without attracting undue attention, Gaspard had "shot" her picture and was packing up his camera again.

"But I don't know what to tell you," Marian protested. "Surely you know all about the gift—it's a memorial to Mrs. Neal's two sons."

"We want something about you—don't be self-conscious—I'm going to fade into the background and stay there," said Richard Groves.

He didn't exactly stay in the background, but he managed to make himself useful. Marian was in demand for several last-minute problems in widely separated sections of the field. Dix cut his finger and came crying in search of her. The Mayor and Mr. Singleton were kept busy seating the arriving honor guests on the huge flag-draped platform—so it was Groves who loaned Marian his pencil for a message, his handkerchief for the wounded Dix and his pocket knife for a light hammer when a strip of the bunting came loose and fluttered its tack wildly in the breeze.

"Don't they give you time to rest before the program begins," he questioned, when the leader of the band had just turned away after a prolonged discussion of the order in which his music should be played, though the selections had been made and approved the week before.

"I'm not tired," said Marian quickly, "but I do wish I could get a drink of water. No, not lemonade—" as Groves started for one of the tables under the trees.

"There's a pump down by the wading pool— the fountain isn't to be turned on till after the dedication. Do you suppose we'll have time to go down there and get a drink before anything begins?"

Richard Groves glanced at his watch.

"Twenty minutes—you can do it easily," he declared.

They hurried down to the pump—which was out of sight of the milling throngs, now trying to establish themselves where they could hear the speeches to be given from the platform—and Groves pumped a gourdful of the clear, cold water for Marian, who drank gratefully, mindful of her white shoes, however.

"I wish I had a picture of you that way," said the reporter appreciatively.

Marian laughed her friendly, unaffected laugh.

"We're Jack and Jill," she smiled.

Groves satisfied his thirst and then began to ask questions at random as he and Marian walked slowly back. She did not realize that she was telling him about herself until she saw the papers the following day—with a large picture of herself and the story of her beautiful mother and artist father and herself, woven into the account of the opening of the playground so cleverly that Marian was fairly bewildered. And when, a few days later, a huge box of chocolates came to her, carrying the card of Richard Groves and inscribed "To little Miss Blessing, whose calmness almost baffled me," Marian wondered why her uncle should seem to be so pleased.

The picturesque ceremonies went smoothly and the crowd applauded the speech-making to the echoes. But when Marian, on behalf of Mrs. Neal, presented the playground to the borough of Stillwell and the Mayor, as the chief executive of the town, received it—well, then the shouting and the stamping and the whistling was something to remember. And when it finally died down and the people scattered to inspect the features and equipment of their new possession, until they should be summoned to the dinner tables set in the broad meadow that was to be the athletic field, Marian relaxed for the first time.

"Wasn't it lovely? Wasn't it perfect?" she urged to Mr. Singleton, who with her uncle was standing on the now deserted platform.

"Yes, you are," said the silver-haired lawyer a little absently.

A rosy blush ran over Marian's face, staining her fair skin up to her blue eyes. Something of the heightened color still remained when she was seated at the head of the honor guest table that night. The flush was the only sign of the inward excitement which possessed her. Outwardly her sweet composure remained unshaken and her smiling eyes sought out the round ones of Dix and Donald and David, grouped near Mr. Singleton at the far end of the table.

"Gee, Marian looks great, doesn't she?" murmured Donald.

But it remained for Mrs. Carey to bestow the crowning happiness. That good woman may forever have remained unconscious of what she did, but Fate willed that she should speak in a tone that carried clearly.

Mr. Singleton had proposed a toast, "to little Miss Blessing, who has shown us what the quiet folk can accomplish in this world," and Marian sat smiling, head a little bent, as the diners at the honor table stood up and table after table followed their example.

Mrs. Carey rose with the rest. She sat at a table to the right of Marian and the faithful Miss Palmer was close beside her. Mrs. Carey's eyes were fixed on Marian's lovely little appealing figure.

"I declare, Hope Palmer," the housekeeper's voice broke the stillness, "I begin to think that Marian looks like her mother, after all!"

THE END